Outside
the Window

Other Books from the Houston Writers Guild

Tides Anthology Series
SkipJack Publishing
Tides of Possibility
Tides of Impossibility

Waves Anthology Series
HWG Press
Waves of Suspense
Waves of Passion
Riding the Waves

Out in the World Anthology Series
HWG Press
Out of Many, One

Outside the Window

the Window

Tales
of the
World

Introduced by

Andrea Barbosa

HOUSTON WRITERS GUILD

PRESS

Outside the Window

Tales of the World

Introduced by

Andrea Barbosa

HOUSTON WRITERS GUILD

PRESS

Contents

Foreword

As Mark Twain so well defined it, "Travel is fatal to prejudice, bigotry, and narrow-mindedness, and many of our people need it sorely on these accounts. Broad, wholesome, charitable views of men and things cannot be acquired by vegetating in one little corner of the earth all one's lifetime."

There are many other wonderful quotes exulting the wonders of traveling. Nowadays, it's especially significant for our need to understand the world and promote empathy between different cultures. By understanding our neighbors, we find ourselves. There are few things as gratifying as seeing the world with our own eyes, experiencing tastes, smells, and sights, making new friends, learning words in different languages, and losing track of time by immersing ourselves in rich history and amazing adventures by wandering our magnificent planet. Each adventure brings a new story, and based on these unique experiences, this anthology was born.

This collection of short stories was put together from the winning entries received for the Outside the Window: Tales of the World contest. Our judges had a hard time choosing from so many talented submissions.

Delight in the unique perspective of these winning stories, where each author crafted their vision by watching outside the window of their experience and creativity to bring us their tales of the world.

Andrea Barbosa
HWG VP and Press Director
Award-winning author/poet

Acknowledgments

The following people were instrumental in the production of this anthology. Throughout its different stages, from organizing and assisting with the contest to the final draft and printed edition, these amazing people generously and selflessly volunteered their time and talent and deserve our sincerest appreciation:

Our panel of judges, who read, rated, gave feedback on, and ranked all the submissions received (see page 137 for more information about these professionals);

Our cover designer, Dylan Drake, who brilliantly conceptualized and designed the beautiful cover for this anthology (page 141);

Our editor and formatter, Dorothy Tinker, who carefully edited and formatted the anthology with professionalism and an eye for detail (page 141);

All members of the Houston Writers Guild Board, who provided much needed and welcome support and feedback through all phases of production.

Queen

Sage Webb

*O*ur building sits on Randolph Street, so cabs are never in short supply. But Yvonne's recent love affair with Lyft has left me standing outside the building, staring at my phone, watching the little car icon that represents Daniyal in a blue Nissan Versa. It creeps toward me and makes a stiff, perfectly ninety-degree left turn. He's getting close.

The little icon exhumes some lost, superannuated memory. As I stare at that tiny car, I'm fifteen again and pulling from beneath the Christmas tree a bright red package with a green bow and a tangle of white, hand-cut snowflakes tied to and hanging from it. After tearing away the paper, I realize my father has made me the first boy in the neighborhood to own Pong. I am happy in a way I have not been happy in a long, long time.

And then I am not. Then I am simply on Randolph Street again.

"Where are you going, sir?" Daniyal asks after the icon arrives in front of my building and I open the door to the Versa.

"Two-fifty-one East Huron. Northwestern Memorial. I thought the phone told you that. It doesn't tell you that?"

"Oh, it tells me. I just like to double-check. Make sure we're all on the same page."

"Oh. Makes sense." I fumble to buckle the seatbelt in a backseat too small to accommodate any properly nourished adult. "It's my first time trying this—Lyft. My wife told me to try it since it's such a short trip. She loves this stuff and keeps pushing me to learn to use it. Says I'll save a fortune."

"Perhaps." He looks at me in the rearview mirror. "Would you like music?" He reaches for the stereo. "What do you like?"

"Oh, I'm fine without it. A little quiet is okay." I inhale canned pine forest and the solitude I interrupted when I slid into the vehicle.

The light turns red and we sit in the blue car in the darkness. Daniyal stares straight out the windshield, his hands at ten and two. I watch a woman on a bike rock back and forth beside my window, her bright red jacket pricking my eyes but also taking me back to that wrapping paper and Pong all those long, long, lost and gone years ago.

The light changes, and Daniyal pulls across the intersection. I shift in my confines.

Yvonne has texted: *You make it into a Lyft.* When she texts, she feels she can omit punctuation. That bothers me.

Yes, I reply. I add, *Very small car.* I want her to know I'm okay for now.

A black hatchback has replaced the bike. In its back window, it has a sticker that reads *Crazy Cat Lady.* I am relieved that silent Daniyal picked me up and not someone with a sticker like that.

"Is the temperature okay? Would you like some more heat?" Daniyal glances up at the mirror again.

"Oh, no. Not at all. Perfectly fine back here. Thank you."

The river gets closer. It should take only three or four minutes to get to the hospital. If everything goes as the doctor said, I should be home by eight. Yvonne will have some wine for me. Maybe she'll let me nip at the Macallan. That nice twenty-one-year-old single malt Marcus gave me for my birthday. I'll feel better after a drink or two.

"Where are you from, Daniyal?" My voice lifts the weight of the car's interior off me a little. "Did you grow up in the city?"

"Oh, no. I'm from Sidon. Lebanon."

"Sidon? I was in Beirut in '82."

Another memory uncurls from its place of slumber.

"Just a wet-behind-the-ears second lieutenant out of Annapolis." I shake my head at this second bit of detritus for the evening.

"It was a bad time," Daniyal says.

Daniyal turns right and we stop. We are sitting in a pool of darkness, with red brake-light water lilies all around us.

"I'm sorry. The bridge is up."

"It appears so, doesn't it? Is it supposed to be up at this hour?"

"I don't think so. I haven't seen it up like this at night, at least not this time of year, that I can remember."

Maybe I should have put some of that Macallan in a flask, but I certainly wasn't expecting this.

"There were things I liked about it over there," I say to the window, watching a pair of women on the sidewalk with shopping bags in their hands and a boy of about ten walking between them. "I liked the music. I listened to a lot of the local music, bought records and brought them back with me. It was good stuff."

Beside us, on the sidewalk, sits a row of dark cubes topped by a sign that reads *Newspapers*. I can't remember the last time I held an actual newspaper. Oh, the terror Pong kicked off.

"I remember listening to a woman singer," I say, trying to remember the name. "Her name was something like Fairuz. I liked her. A lot. Very pretty voice."

"You know Fairuz?" Daniyal's eyes look back from the mirror again.

"Yes. I liked her. I remember a song—" I have to stop and think, as with recalling the woman singer's name.

I turn from the window and the landscape of the obsolete newspaper rack to place my hand against my jaw and temple. "It was called—" It takes me a minute. At first, I can only see that circle bouncing back and forth between the Pong paddles. Then I am outside a bar in the hinterlands of Anne Arundel County. And then I remember.

"It was called *'Habaytak Bisayf.'* Am I saying that right?"

"*'Habaytak Bisayf'*? Yes, perfectly. That is one of my favorite songs. They say she has the voice of an angel." Now it's Daniyal's smile that fills the mirror.

"Yes, that song is very beautiful."

This was supposed to be a five-minute ride. Yet somehow it has taken me back to Lebanon, and I am a twenty-two-year-old kid again, and it's all so, so far back: Back before all the nonsense, the anger, the infidelities big and small on both sides; long before Yvonne and the occasional description of "second wife." Back before what they call success, and long, long before unrecognized, undiagnosed *anythings* lying in wait in brain tissue and heartbreaks. Back closer to the happiness of Pong and love songs and memories of home. I am newly wed to Margaret—azure-eyed Margaret of quick temper and languid seduction—and full of hope and plans.

Outside the Versa, a young man balances on one of those so-called hoverboards, bags of what I think are groceries slung over his shoulders. I remember how I thought it romantic and gallant to carry Margaret's picture in my pocket through Beirut, how that first kiss tingled and breathed when I returned home, how I told her she had seen the Levant from my pocket.

"What other music do you listen to?" I ask Daniyal.

"Queen. I love Queen. We will rock you!"

"Freddie Mercury. He was talented. Creative."

"Oh, yes," Daniyal says.

"I should have listened to more Queen in the eighties. It's good stuff." I sigh. "Would've been better than all that Lebanese music I brought back. My daughter got old enough to put those records on, and now she dances at restaurants down in South Bend. If it'd been Queen, maybe she would've played volleyball or tennis."

"Your daughter dances to Lebanese music?"

"Yes." I sigh a second time and shake my head. "She performs dinner shows at Middle Eastern restaurants. She's going to school down there but spends all my money on custom-made costumes from Turkey and traveling all over to take dance workshops. She dances to that woman Fairuz's songs. I've seen her, but I don't like it. Something about it makes me uncomfortable.

"Her stepmom loves it, though. Sabrina—my daughter—she didn't get along with Yvonne—my wife—at first. Sabrina was upset I'd remarried. But it was time. Now the two of them are right as rain. Yvonne drives down there and takes the dance workshops Sabrina teaches. Yvonne's all into the whole silly thing too."

I hear Daniyal chuckle.

"Would you like to hear *'Habaytak Bisayf'*? I have it here." He touches his phone.

"Sure."

"Be ayam el bard, be ayam el sheti." That voice fills the Versa. *"We el raseef bohayra, we el sharea gharee'a."*

"I know it's a love song," I say. "Someone told me once what it means, but I don't remember. What does it mean?"

"It's winter. Cold. And the sidewalks are flooded like a lake," Daniyal answers. "This girl is waiting for him. He told her to wait, but he has gone away. He's forgotten her, but she is pining for him. She loved him in the summer and waited for him in the winter. His eyes are summer. Hers are winter. And their reunion, 'oh my love,' is beyond summer and beyond winter."

He clears his throat.

"A stranger passes and gives her a message," he continues translating. Then another cough. "The boy wrote it with his tears. The message, the letters of it, were lost. The days passed. The years made them strangers. And winter erased the letters in the message."

He tries to clear his throat yet again, blows his nose on a tissue from the colored, patterned box sitting on the passenger seat, and then lifts a bottle of water from that seat. The voice from the phone fades and then rises again in a new rhythm with a new story.

"Sad," I say.

"Yes, very sad."

"It sounds sad even just listening to it—not even knowing the words."

"It was my wife's favorite song," Daniyal says. "She sang along, and I always had to tell her to stop—that I would never leave her or write her messages without letters in them. But she would laugh and keep singing and dance in circles. Not like your daughter." He tries to laugh. "Just in our home."

He pauses, takes another sip of water from the bottle. "But once she danced on the beach. Did you ever go to Sidon?"

"Yes, actually, I did once."

"You saw the castle on the sea?"

"Yes, the crusaders' fortress. Yes, I remember that." I see myself, a young Marine officer, watching the sun set behind a medieval castle on the Mediterranean, Margaret's picture in my pocket.

"You know what, Daniyal, would you mind putting on a little more heat back here now?"

"Of course."

"Thank you."

"The castle is beautiful, is it not?" Daniyal's hands rub up and down the steering wheel, fingers flexing in and out.

"Yes, very impressive."

"We were there one evening when we were kids. Just married. Young and happy, and she danced and sang. She danced on the sand. She had her arms flung out." Daniyal imitates a gesture of abandon.

He takes another drink of water.

"She—my wife—had long black hair, like the sky over the sea at night."

I see him turn and look out at the walk along the river and at the bridge. I know he sees his wife dancing on the beach some long-lost night ago. He wheezes against the nagging grip on his throat and blows his nose again. I pretend not to notice why.

"We—we had the *Ginnaz*, the prayers, and then the bread forty days after that," he says, eyes and attention on the other side of the window, of the world. "I pray she is with our Holy Mother."

The Versa has warmed up, perhaps too much now, and the only thing I can say is "I'm sorry for your loss." The tone of my voice is too low.

"Oh, no. This is life. Death is a part of life."

"She was very young?" I don't know why I ask.

"Twenty when she was struck and went into the coma," he replies. "We had gone to Beirut because she was having some sickness we could not explain. We thought we could do better at a hospital in Beirut, and my uncle told us to come stay with his family there. But then the Israeli bombing started. You know how it was. You were there. And she was walking one day—"

He robs the box of another of its white squares of Kleenex. "Excuse me."

"Oh, no. And you don't have to—"

"No, it is good to remember," he insists. "She had just turned twenty-two when she left us. I sat with her every day. We read together: poems and scripture and stories. She loved to read."

He smiles into that mirror.

"And I sang to her. I sang her Fairuz. Every day, we were together. My uncle took care of me, and I went to the hospital every day."

The block has returned to his throat.

"She never woke up after the bomb. But it didn't matter. I just wanted to sit beside her. The last day, that afternoon, I was reading to her, and you know . . . ." He looks at me in the mirror, waits to catch my eyes with his. "She squeezed my hand. Truly. I was holding her hand, and she squeezed mine tightly, and then she was gone. I pray God lets me take that memory to my own deathbed."

He crosses himself, touching his right shoulder and then his left.

The Nissan is quiet.

Outside the windows, we see the bridge start to lower.

"Yvonne is Catholic," I blurt out. "I'll tell her to say a prayer. It is good to pray for the dead. What was your wife's name?"

"Marina." He inhales and exhales a few times. "Thank you."

"Yvonne will light a candle on Sunday."

"Thank you."

The bridge finds its mate from the other side of the river, and the traffic loosens, the knot of cars released to flow and rediscover their rhythm.

From the river, it is only a few minutes to the hospital. Daniyal pulls up in front of the doors to which I direct him.

"Wait," he says as I begin to thank him for the ride. "Are you ill? Are you here because you are ill? I'll park and walk in with you."

He presses the button on his dash to activate his hazard lights.

"You shouldn't go in alone. No one should go to a hospital alone." He turns the car off and opens his door.

"Oh, no, thank you, but I'm only going in to attend to some paperwork," I tell him. "No need to worry, but I do appreciate your kindness. Thank you."

"Okay then. Good luck, and listen to Fairuz once in a while, and then to Freddie Mercury and Queen." He smiles into the mirror a last time, and I catch him catching something in my face.

"Here, sir." He reaches for his box and hands me a tissue I hadn't realized I needed. He keeps looking. "Here," he repeats and hands me the box.

"Thank you." I grope to connect with the box and take it from him without looking up from where my other hand rests on the inside of the car door. "Thank you for the ride. And the music."

I shut the door of the Nissan and approach the hospital entrance, the windows in the gray building amber in the night. I haven't been here in a long time, and maybe the light of the windows isn't amber. Maybe it's marigold or saffron. Regardless, it's the color of a world I have avoided for a long, long time. But this is the last time.

On the other side of the windows, I follow the doctor's white coat down a hallway. Margaret lies in the bed, as she has for nineteen months. The ball of the world has bounced back and forth between the paddles of man's machinations, but nothing true or real has altered the monochrome, the antiseptic scent of affliction, the simple shapes on the screen of existence. The ventilator makes Margaret's chest rise and fall. The doctor hands me a clipboard and I nod and sign. The Kleenex box dangles in my left hand as I pass the board back; I don't want to use the tissues, so I don't try to speak. I am sure I am gone and out of the building before Margaret is gone. It is very dark now and I walk toward St. Clair Street.

On Sunday, I'll ask Yvonne to light two candles. She'll understand.

On St. Clair, I flag down a cab for the trip home.

ARTHUR PIKE

*T*he day his mother returned, Hap Jackson sat on the metal steps that bridged the dirt and the trailer where he lived. He studied the day, the sun edging toward noon, and closer to hand, the jerk and dart of lizards in the weeds.

Hap measured the size of his world first by that trailer. From there, it was all up. From the little trailer to the Peterbilt 389 dump truck to the big triangle of the Link-Belt excavator out back and then, higher still, to the mountains against the New Mexico sky. Somewhere between Hap and the sky was his father and the rock hills where he dug a living out of the gravel.

That day, Hap caught a noise from the south, one beyond the thrum of the excavator at work. He sighted a car at play on the dirt road. It was yellow and high-fendered, with a sign on its roof. As it came closer, he could make out the *On Duty* backlit on that sign.

This was a novelty. They were seldom visited and then only by hollowed-out men in caved-in trucks come for loads of slag. A yellow car carried some other meaning entirely. Hap charged down the stairs, stood for a moment to verify the sight, and then took out toward the back to alert his father.

In all his nine years, Hap had found no sensation to compare to running. He loved the feel of his body at work, feet to knee to thigh, sinew and torque. He was good at it, and he applied his skill now to the flat patch to be covered to reach his father.

His father sat high on the rough track of the Link-Belt, which idled like a winded beast at his back. He was dousing his thirst from a gallon jug of water.

"Company," Hap yelled on approach. "On the road."

His father looked at his watch. "No one picking up today."

Hap's father was short, compact, hard cut from what appeared to be the same earth he dug a living from. A crew cut burred his scalp, his eyes creased in a perpetual squint, and he stayed clean-shaven by daily habit. Muscle featured prominently across most surfaces of his body.

"Not a truck." Hap swung back toward the road. "A yellow car."

Out front, Hap and his father watched the cab idle some yards down the road. Hap had never seen anything so bright and high shine that wasn't in the sky. His father rubbed grime from his hands with a rag, preparing to transact whatever business might pertain.

Soon enough, the back door of the cab opened. From the revealed darkness, a woman emerged, slight and bob-haired. She came determinedly across the space between them, eyes forward, ignoring stumbles caused by rocks and sand. A few yards from them, she set herself, hands to hips.

"You're not welcome here." His father had stiffened at first sight of her. He smacked dust off his pants legs in her general direction.

The woman shifted from foot to foot to avoid the airborne dirt. "Didn't think I would be."

Wind waffled over the tires that anchored the trailer roof. The sun was a bright lamp shining in their faces. Still, Hap could make out her contours. She had a good high forehead, curling-iron hair, sky-blue eyes that held their own, and a toothy mouth fixed on mean. Hap remembered the old photo album buried deep within the trailer. He'd seen this face before. This, then, was his mother.

She gathered her uncertainty and worked it into a look of pride. "I've come to see my child."

"Your child?" His father was spitting now.

She firmed her back. "My son."

"I'll say it again," his father said. "You're not welcome here."

"I got rights."

"You left them behind when you took off out of here four years ago."

"Be that as it may—"

"With not a glance behind you."

Words shot between them like pellets. Hap took cover in a distraction: the driver of the car that had brought his mother. That man lifted himself out of the vehicle (labeled *Checker Cab*) and stretched in the sun. He was tall—he had a head or more on Hap's father—deep black, and thin as cards. He scratched his nearly bald head furiously with both hands before shouting across the distance, "Meter's running."

Hap came back to his father and mother, both of which had worked themselves into cold frenzies.

"We could talk child support. We could talk alimony," she said.

"We could," he yelled. "But we won't."

"I'll be back." Tears and spit flew from his mother.

"No, you won't." His father pawed the dirt, searching for an anchor point.

"I'm bringing lawyers next time." She stomped toward the cab, hands raised, middle fingers flying, ankles twisting in the loose-packed dirt.

"You do that." His father punched the air with an index finger and kicked a plume of dust at her.

"We'll have our time, Hap," his mother called over her shoulder. "Never you worry."

"He ain't worried." His father roostered dirt out behind him and rounded on Hap. "You. Inside until she's good and gone."

Inside, Hap watched the cab recede into the distance. The trailer filled with the punch of the Link-Belt, gunned by his angry father. Hap considered the shape the day had assumed. He didn't much remember his mother; she didn't come up in conversation within the trailer. Hap knew kids who came equipped with a full set of parents but had found his father was good enough for whatever purpose parents served. Still, he couldn't deny some curiosity.

The dust cloud from the cab lingered on the horizon, immune to the crosscutting winds. As he watched, it grew, thickening rather than dispersing. Soon enough, he saw the yellow cab traveling back up the road.

He jumped the steps and ran, pumping toward the road as the cab swung in, rolled up close, and turned in a few feet from him. The backdoor window slid down; his mother was beaming out at him.

"Ever been in a cab, Hap?"

Hap Jackson didn't know how rich people lived, but he imagined the inside of that cab was a close approximation. It was spacious and dim and smelled of world travel. The high bench he shared with his mother was worn smooth, and a thick plastic panel separated them from the driver. Through it, Hap sighted the dash, bristling with dials and knobs, a crackling radio, and a red-numbered fare counter.

They rolled down the road at what Hap judged to be walking speed, the engine barely idling. "I don't like this." The driver's voice was so deep as to be near inaudible.

Hap stared at a snapshot of the driver in the panel behind the driver's seat. It showed a round face set against a white background. A line of black fuzz, no longer present on the actual man, rode his upper lip. His ears were tight against his head, and his forehead peaked under a stiff dusting of hair. He looked startled.

"What's that?" His mother watched the trailer recede through the back window of the cab.

"Taking this boy away. I don't like it," the big driver said.

"Don't like it?" His mother rolled a smile Hap's way. "Do you like it?"

Hap bounced a bit on the big seat, felt the springs flexing under him. "Yes."

"All good back here," his mother told the driver, triumphant.

"I don't believe the father would share your sense of well-being," the driver said.

His mother waved a hand in front of her nose. "A joyless man."

The cab barely rolled along the dirt road. Static cracked and spit from the radio. The fare counter incremented.

"Can you imagine? Seven years old and trapped in that life?" His mother nodded back up the road.

"Nine," said Hap.

"This boy needs a joyride," his mother said. "Right, Hap?"

"I'm nine years old."

The driver cranked himself around in his seat to glare at the two of them. The cab drifted forward, bound for thicker gravel at road's edge. Hap's mother sliced off a thick wedge of smile and tipped her head significantly toward Hap, who bounced a bit more on the smooth vinyl of his seat.

The cab driver growled and turned back to the controls. He straightened their glide and scratched first one side then the other of his scalp. Then they picked up speed on the washboard, bound for Albuquerque. Hap pressed into the deep give of his seat.

They were rolling past ranks of billboards on the edge of town before his mother spoke again. "Manners," she chirped. "Hap, this is Atlas Taveez. And Mr. Altas, this is Happy Jackson. Hap, in the familiar."

Hap exchanged a stony glance with Atlas in the rearview mirror. "Hap's naming has a two-fold meaning," his mother continued. "First, he was such a happy, happy child. Bright as day. Second, he made his father and I so very, very glad."

That last ran counter to Hap's vague memories of his mother and father. He remembered a wealth of arguments: His mother calling his father a rock hound. Him calling her a gold digger. Regardless of subject matter, those spats had always proceeded along geologic lines.

"Atlas and Hap. Hap and Atlas. Makes you want to sing." She sat back in her seat, smiling, satisfied. Then, she surged forward again. "Do you know where Mr. Atlas is from, Hap? Originally?"

"No, I don't," Hap said.

"Africa," she said, victorious.

"What part?" Hap directed his question at the round badge face on the back of the seat.

"Rhodesia," his mother said, sustaining her triumphant tone.

"Zimbabwe," Mr. Atlas muttered.

"You know where Africa is?" Hap's mother asked.

Hap didn't. He imagined it was south of the road they were currently on. "Yes," he said.

His mother ignored his answer. "Africa is a large country in the lower half of the world. As to Rhodesia, or Zimbabwe as Mr. Atlas prefers, if we imagine Africa as a face, with the Mediterranean Sea as sweat on its brow, Zimbabwe might be the nose." She tweaked Hap's nose with her thumb. "Although somewhat off-center, given Africa's asymmetry."

Up front, Atlas sighed heavily.

"How do you know?" Hap scuffed her touch off his nose.

"I know because I teach. Geography. The science of countries and their neighbors. My great passion. Giving children some sense of the size of the world they don't know."

The car chunked beneath their feet, and the ride smoothed out and quieted. They'd left the dirt road for paved. The loose suburbs of Albuquerque tightened around them. Traffic lights blinked at intersections. Atlas shouldered the cab ahead.

"And you'll be taking this happy boy where?" he asked.

"Let's just drive." His mother crinkled her nose at Hap and gave a shiver of pleasure.

"I do not just drive," Atlas said.

His mother stiffened. "Yes, well." She studied the mixed-use landscape slipping by. "Your business is very destination-oriented, isn't it?"

Atlas backed off the gas. The cab slowed, kinking traffic.

"A shame." His mother's words spilled into the air. "Stifles improvisation."

The cab coasted toward a full stop; impatience flared inside and out. "Destination, please," the driver snapped. Horns peeled about them. "Immediately."

"All right, all right," his mother said, frantic. "Pull in here."

Atlas left the angry traffic for the parking lot of a giant building with *Shop for Less* blazing in man-high letters over the entrance.

"Perfect." His mother's tension eased as suddenly as it had flared. "Gentlemen, welcome to Shop for Less. My current employer."

"What happened to school teacher?" Atlas's glare filled the rearview.

His mother addressed Hap. "Mr. Atlas wouldn't know this because he's new to our country—"

"I've lived in Albuquerque for twenty-five years," he barked.

"But a school teacher can't make it on just one job. Drop me at the front door." She waved across the lot at the store entrance, where a funnel of shoppers was draining inward.

"This will result in my fare being paid, how?" Atlas asked.

"Via my paycheck," his mother said. "Which is waiting inside to be picked up."

Atlas swiveled in his seat and brought his face to the gap in the plastic divider, mouth set in a hard line. Hap's mother met him, grim for grim.

Hap pressed against his window. His father shopped at a convenience store. It was a small, pinched place of narrow aisles and dusty product lines. Carts there were squeaky and crabbed, fit for the items his father filled them with: macaroni and cheese, pickle loaf, tots, and fish sticks caked with frost. He turned to his mother. "Take me with you."

"Of course, Hap. It would be a joy." Victorious, she turned to the driver. "Right, Mr. Atlas?"

Atlas held his stand for a minute more, then sighed and reached for the wheel. "I'll come in with you," he said, pulling up to the entrance.

His mother fired up her dignity. "I'd thank you to allow us a few private mother/son moments. Right, Hap?"

"Can we go in now?" Hap asked.

Atlas stuck his face to the gap in the plastic. "I'll be here," he growled. "Watching that door."

Inside, Hap felt the whole of the world opening up. The concrete floor planed off into distant expanses, smoothly polished and sheening under blazing light fixtures. The air murmured with the sound of a dozen tongues and smelled of exotic fruit. His fellow shoppers pressed on into the experience, guiding extra large carts, while Hap was stopped in his tracks.

His mother had walked ahead a few yards; she turned back to him. "Never been in a big box store?"

"If that's what this is, no," he said.

She took him by the arm, and he let her guide him toward the store's Vision Center. A wall of eyeglasses met them—lenses in a dozen different shapes backlit and glowing like masks, eyes there yet not there. Hap searched out the largest pair within his reach and maneuvered it onto his face, its pads wide on his nose. Things looked brighter, more vivid. He turned to show his mother, just in time to catch her slipping a pair of dark sunglasses between the top two buttons of her blouse.

She walked toward him. "As if you need more eyes than you already have." She lifted the glasses from his face and set them back on the display. "Onward."

Down the store's wide main aisle they tracked, dodging carts and browsers, moving briskly past mountain ranges of no-brand jeans and cliffs of marked-down hoodies. The booze section spread out away from them, oceans of dark red and white wine. They entered a chilled section of open-mouthed coolers and tall refrigeration units, filled with packets of meat, fish, pastries, and fruits. Shoppers lifted hunks of wrapped red meat and tossed them into their carts. Men in blood-smeared white aprons wielded knifes. Hap's mother led him through the cacophony, to a large room labeled *Fresh Produce*. Mist trained out from the entrance.

"Deep breath now," she said as she led him in.

Hap did as he was told. A blast of cold air met them. They exited the temperate zone for the arctic. Shoppers moved quickly, pulling sweaters close. The walls were stacked with pallets of fruits and vegetables—baby carrots, asparagus, romaine hearts—all foreign to him. His mother picked through a five-foot-high display of red grapes, broke off a stem's worth, and began eating. Hap palmed a red snowball of a pomegranate. His mother led them through Fresh Produce, nipping a fruit here and a vegetable there, and out to the relative warmth of the meat and poultry section.

"What have we here?" she asked.

They came to a stand where an employee in a hairnet monitored a bubbling crockpot of something edible.

"Curry," the employee said. A display packet of the stuff—orange mud embedded with chunks of white meat—leaned against the crockpot. "Chicken curry."

"My favorite." His mother took a sample for herself and handed one to Hap. "From the Indian subcontinent." She took a dainty bite.

"New Jersey," the attendant said.

"Originally," his mother said between chews.

Hap scooped a helping into his mouth. Curry tasted like seasoned grit. His mother reached for seconds.

"One per customer," the employee said.

His mother snagged two more samples before the employee could ward her off. "He's a growing boy."

"One per customer." The employee shielded the remaining samples from further incursions.

His mother handed him another helping of the stuff and marched them away.

Hap chewed his way through the second helping. "I'm not growing that much."

"I won't abide stinginess."

They came to a zone of quietness then, deep in the store, given over to drinks. Pallets formed canyons around them, stacked high with cartoned and bottled juices: apple, pineapple, orange, and red and white grape. Plastic-wrapped packages of bottled water, a great inland sea of contained liquid, rose over Hap's head.

"Here we are." His mother waved her arm, indicating the territory they'd entered. "At the very end of the big-box world." She punched a hole in the plastic of a carton of water bottles, pulled one clear, took a slug, and handed it to him.

Hap washed the liquid around in his mouth to evacuate the curry. It was tasteless, smooth, and skin temperature, not like the water at home, which smacked of roots. He glanced at the label, then returned the bottle to her.

"Well," she said. "We've had a time, haven't we?"

"A big-box time," he said.

Her laugh wasn't quite what it had been before. "Mark me, though," she said. "I told your father I'd be back, and I was."

"Yes, ma'am," he said. "I suppose you're right."

She jabbed at him with the water bottle. "Where do you get 'suppose' from? I surely did come back. As promised."

"In a manner of speaking," Hap said.

She set hands to her hips, spilling a dollop of water to the concrete. "Hap Jackson. You see me standing right in front of you, don't you?"

"Yes, ma'am."

"Then you'd have to agree I came back," she said.

"I understood that staying's a part of coming back," he said.

In the dim light at the end of that world, he saw that his mother was, in her own way, as tired and frantic as his father was. The weariness was plain. Hap wondered about this worn-outness he encountered in adults, wondered if it came on suddenly like a dose of food poisoning or if it snuck up on a person over time.

She'd gone hard, especially in the eyes. The smile was still on her lips, but it was missing everywhere else. She'd lost something. Interest, he figured.

"Chipper little thing, aren't you?" she said.

"I don't know what that means," he said.

She didn't bother to explain. "I'm going to fetch my check from the office." She waved a hand vaguely toward some area to her right. "As promised to Mr. Atlas. You run and find him. I'll join you in due course."

Hap sighted down the long concourse that ran the length of the store, thick with displays, counters, and slow-moving shoppers. It thrilled him. He turned back to her and plucked the pilfered sunglasses from her blouse. She'd told him to run. So he did.

He came out of the blocks quickly. He was used to the chink and chip of mixed gravel; the smooth concrete floor here was conducive to speed. He flowed out of the cool zone, into a space where furniture items were sold, rabbiting along. Beyond the massage chair demonstration, he swerved past a snarl of carts at discount books. He surged through the drug section. He soared between the narrow aisles of bagged candies, cookies, and nuts.

Checkout loomed before him, aisles full and carts backed up all down the line. He veered west, toward the express lanes; few came here for just ten items. Sighting an opening, he executed a turn, rubber soles squeaking. As he threaded the needle, baskets swung in his wake. The exit was next, clogged with satisfied consumers. He pushed the shades deep into his pocket and lit his boosters, emulating his mother's approach—low and fast, under the radar.

Then he was outside. Thickening crowds swirled, their Saturday shopping accomplished. Up above, pigeons perched on the high arcs of the letters of the store's sign. He felt like shouting, bragging at full volume about the run he'd just delivered. Instead, he panted. The bright light of day cut at his eyes. He dug the sunglasses out, popped them on, tightening them to his nose, and moved like a king into the brown-tinted day.

Atlas had been watching for them, and he dodged the crowd toward him, all long legs and big strides. "Where is she?" Atlas stood over Hap, a pillar blocking the sun.

Hap broke the news a piece at a time. "Getting her check." He nudged the slipping shades back up his nose.

Atlas swung his enormous head in close to Hap's. His breath was massive, his voice a hot blast. "Where is she?"

There was nothing for it. "She's gone," Hap said.

Atlas unfurled and bellowed. He launched himself into the

pulsing, swarming crowd, striding hard and disappearing with the throngs through that inviting front entrance.

Hap had been a few minutes in the backseat of the cab before Atlas returned, stalking through the multitude, scratching his scalp. Atlas pounded across to the cab, yanked the door open, and ducked to bring his sweating face level with Hap's. "Get out of my cab."

Hap nodded gravely and stepped clear. Atlas slammed the door. Then he made the round of the vehicle, kicking the tires, pounding fists on the top, slapping the hood, open handed, yelling at the sky. A crowd gathered to watch him rant, leaning on their carts, amused, as if this too were part of the big-box experience. Hap stood by, hands clasped behind his back, awaiting the next steps.

Finally, the big man ran himself down. He leaned over the hood of his cab, head hung and sweating. After a few moments' rest, he lifted himself erect, turned away from the sun, and found the crowd watching. He grunted and flung his arm at them as if to wipe the slate clean. Then Atlas lowered his gaze to Hap.

"Get in my cab," he snapped.

They made their surge-and-skid way back through Albuquerque, Atlas taking his frustration out on the cab and his fellow drivers: pounding the wheel, ripping from lane to lane, laying hard on the horn, running yellows and reds. Once they'd cleared the blacktop, Atlas fishtailed across the dirt road, ran the shoulder, and took out the occasional prickly pear.

Hap discretely buckled his seatbelt. He let some time and energy elapse before he delivered more bad news. "My father won't pay you."

Atlas grimaced in the rearview mirror. "Then he won't get you back."

Hap rolled this possibility over in his mind. It seemed unlikely, but the meter on the dash had now turned over to triple digits.

"I apologize," Atlas said, calmer now. "That woman." He yanked his sun visor down to shield his eyes from the afternoon's advanced light.

Hap remembered the walls of the trailer, resounding with arguments in his younger days. "I could wash your car," he said.

"Man, I've wasted a day. I need money. I don't need my car washed."

"I disagree. It's dirty," Hap said.

They rode in silence. The day deepened. The crunchy road came and went. Hap nudged the glasses up his nose and smudged a lick of dust off the plastic cover on Atlas's picture. "Your picture's a lot younger than you," Hap said.

Atlas grunted, lifted his shoulders, and held them up for a moment before dropping them. For all his size, Hap thought he seemed rumpled.

"You miss it," Hap said.

"Miss what?" Atlas asked.

"Rhodesia. Zimbabwe."

Atlas closed his eyes, heavy lids blocking white light. Hap waited for the whites to reappear. When they did, Atlas spoke. "My country is known for evil governance and a great waterfall."

What Hap knew of water amounted to his father's ancient garden hose and the Rio Grande running weakly down the valley. "What waterfall?" he asked.

"Victoria Falls. We share it with Zaire. You've surely seen pictures?"

Hap had not. "I have not," he said.

"The largest waterfall in the world. Vast, vast." Atlas smoothed the air to indicate great volumes of water flowing.

"What's it like?"

"Imagine a place that's the opposite of this." Atlas nodded at the road ahead and all the dry world beyond.

Hap set his feet firmly on the floor, clasped his hands in his lap, and closed his eyes behind the shades. No luck. He had no ground to imagine anything other than what he knew.

"Replace these flat lands with cliffs. These shrubs become great trees. And always, always water, falling always, chasing itself."

"What's it there for?" Hap asked.

"There for?" Atlas twisted in his seat to look at Hap, then slapped his hand against the wheel. "It's not there for anything. It's the natural world."

"Yes," Hap said. "But what's it there for in that particular place?"

Atlas waved the buzzing fly of Hap's question away. "There's a river flowing. It meets a cliff. There's no option."

Hap nodded and let the explanation lie, unsatisfying as it was. The quiet was lit by the churn of tire on dirt and the squelch of the radio.

Then: "When I was a child," Atlas said, "perhaps your age . . ."

"Nine," Hap said.

"Perhaps." Atlas rubbed his chin as if memories were stored there. "My parents took us to the falls. There were paths up the cliffs. Slippery. Treacherous. But once at the top, with all the water rushing, right there across the table as it were, the mist would descend on you. Your hair. Your arms. You could lift your face to it . . ."

Atlas turned his head to the view out his window. They hit a rough patch; rocks, thrown up by the cab's tires, pinged and cracked off the undercarriage. Hap saw a jet streaming overhead, hooking left for some point south.

"I told you," Hap said. "You miss that place."

Atlas turned back to face front, focused on the washboard and the bounce of the cab as they passed over it. "I barely remember it."

Hap nodded. "I don't know what that's like. To miss someplace. I've always been home."

Right on time, the trailer emerged from a plume of red dust ahead. Hap's father stood watch at the top of the stairs, phone headset in one hand, cradle in the other. He hung up the phone and set it on the step as Atlas turned the cab onto the dirt in front of the trailer.

At the end of the line, Hap and Atlas each drew a breath and reached for their doors. Hap ran to his father and impacted him hard as he came down the steps. Atlas stepped his way toward the two of them, waiting his turn.

"Where the hell have you been?" His father's voice was hard but for the squeak at the question mark.

"Big box store," Hap said. "Mom took me."

"*Took* being the operative word," his father said. "And with no permission given." He laid hands on Hap's shoulders and shook him a bit. "You understand?"

Hap looked into the hard, creased land of his father's face and felt the stiffness of calluses on his shoulders. He did understand, although that had no particular bearing on his sense of a day well lived. "Yes."

Hap's father turned his focus to Atlas. At the sight of Atlas's height, Hap's father set his back and dug his feet into the ground. "You should've known better." He jabbed a finger at the big man.

Atlas met this impassively. "I'm an open-access carrier," he said. "I don't ask questions."

"There's your first problem."

"Be that as it may," Atlas said. "The fare owed is one hundred ten dollars."

"I'm not obligated to honor any debt of hers," Hap's father said.

"I wasn't obligated to return the boy," Atlas said.

A sun-filled and dusty standoff ensued. Hap observed the tenseness between them, unsure how the tie would be broken. In the end, Atlas cracked the stone.

"There is another way."

Through what was left of that great afternoon, as he filled buckets with dishwashing liquid and scrubbed the big fenders and bumper of the cab and polished its yellow surfaces, Hap had the feeling he was running, even if he wasn't. Atlas and his father sat in their lawn chairs in the reflections off the cab, gave directions, sipped their beers, and laughed together over subjects that meant little to Hap.

What did mean something was when Atlas took the hose to help him rinse. The big man arced the stream just past Hap's head. Drops peppered his new sunglasses and the mist fell on his face, and he knew then just how home felt.

A Sari in the Desert

MONICA BERRY

When she came to visit us from New Delhi, I never wanted Mama, my Hindu grandmother, to walk me through the empty lot to Hubert Humphrey Elementary School.

It was 1984. Tumbleweeds still dotted our neighborhood shortcut. But the unfortunate and all-too-common New Mexican landscaping foes didn't worry me. Mama could handle a weed or three. She could handle much more. She'd grown up in Lucknow, India, and often recounted to us stories of playing in the gardens near her childhood home.

"Once, a long snake with white and black scales crawled right by my feet," Mama told us. "I could see the snake's tongue. It was hissing! Then the gardener saw it before it could bite me! He raised his huge knife and swung it down hard. He cut the snake in half!" she bragged.

Consequently, I knew that Mama's historical feats over potentially poisonous reptiles trumped any number of camouflaged lizards we might encounter among the prickly, dried-up plants. I just didn't want Mama to escort me to school, regardless of the route.

My Indian-born Hindu father and American-born Jewish mother had already made my life prone to taunting questions from inquisitive classmates: "You don't go to church on Sundays?"; "Why does your dad talk funny?"; "Why does your house smell like spices all the time?"; "Why don't you celebrate Christmas?"

By the time I turned six years old, I'd come to feeble terms with defending my culturally and religiously different family. I had pat answers for most of my classmates' questions:

"No, we go to temple for Friday night services, or sometimes on Saturday mornings. We have Sunday school on Sundays, just like you do."

"Because he was born in India and went to school in England."

"My dad likes to make curry. It's what Indian people eat. The smell goes away if you open a window while he's cooking."

"We celebrate a Jewish holiday around Christmas time. It lasts for eight days, and I get to open a new present every night!"

My first-grade classmates didn't appreciate my explanations. And they looked horrified when Santa Claus didn't appear during the Hanukkah miracle of the oil lasting for the eight nights.

"Mom, why do I have to keep telling the Hanukkah story? Why am I the only one who knows it?" I asked.

"There aren't any other Jewish kids in your class," Mom told me. "Most of the kids celebrate Christmas. They don't know the story of the Maccabees. You have to be the storyteller."

"But I don't want to be the only Jewish kid! It's lonely. And the other kids don't get the story. They think our holiday is stupid."

That comment stirred something in Mom. Next thing I knew, she and the mother of Josh Kronberg, the other Jewish kid in first grade, petitioned Principal Romero. They wanted Josh and me in the same second-grade class.

After several meetings, the principal agreed. The next school year, my name and Josh's appeared on Ms. Seaman's class list. I finally had an ally.

Well, I had half an ally. Josh and I fielded all the Jewish questions together. But he offered no help with the Indian ones.

So why in the world would I have wanted to advertise my devoutly Hindu, Indian-accented, sari-wearing, bindi-foreheaded, and nose-pierced grandma to the schoolyard mob on my daily trips to and from elementary school?

In hindsight, those thoughts ring shameful, deplorable really, in my mind. However, I've had thirty-plus years to reflect on them. The most embarrassing part of my story is that I felt that way about my own grandmother. How could I feel ashamed about Mama's clothes? Her colorful silk saris, in all their blues, pinks, and greens, accented with gold-threaded borders, were each six yards of amazing handiwork—not to mention pricy exhibitions of the highest fashion and latest styles in her native India.

And how could I feel ashamed of the way Mama spoke English? Years before, she had accepted that Dad would never move home to India, that he wouldn't have an arranged marriage, and that she wouldn't have an Indian or even Hindu daughter-in-law. Mama didn't dispense any guilt toward Dad or show even an inkling of hurt. She just opened her welcoming mind, arms, and heart.

Mama learned English to communicate with her daughter-in-law and granddaughters. She practiced writing it in her weekly letters, which she sent via thin light-blue aerograms to Mom. She always double underlined her capitalized block letters spelling BY AIRMAIL on the front, below our Albuquerque address. Meanwhile, Papa, my grandfather, would speak to her in English, rather than Hindi, in their Indian home.

"Let's speak more English!" he'd encourage. "Then we can talk to Monica and Sheila on the phone. And we'll be ready to greet them when we get to America."

Mama worked hard to make sure we would all understand each other when we were together. Then she traveled to the New Mexico desert because she loved Sheila and me. She flew thousands of miles to help Dad take care of us after our mother's leukemia diagnosis. Within days of my parents' decision to seek the best cancer treatment for Mom and admit her to a hospital in Seattle, Mama had obtained an extended tourist visa for travel to the US.

While Dad worked during the week and traveled every weekend to see Mom and to stay on top of her doctors and her disease, Mama took care of us. She never complained that Sheila and I didn't speak Hindi. She never chastised us for wanting to eat less spicy dishes than she and Dad did. Instead, she smiled and cooked two separate pots of lentils for dinner.

Despite her Hindu faith and vegetarianism, Mama never refused to make our American meals. She didn't balk at the deli meat we kept in the refrigerator, though it represented a terrible affront to her deities. Every time she touched roast beef to make sandwiches for my school lunches or boiled a hotdog for Sheila's afternoon snack, Mama violated countless Hindu tenets. But she kept the shame to herself. Sacrificing part of her beliefs for the gratification and happiness of her granddaughters became a tradeoff Mama was pleased to make over and over again.

Mama also made friends with our neighbors and started delivering hot dishes of *saag paneer* and *moong dal* to them. Some of our native New Mexican pals even requested she prepare her five-alarm-fire spicy meals. Their taste buds could handle the heat.

Often, Sheila and I couldn't remember the names of Mama's gods.

"What's the blue one's name?" I asked.

"Krishna," Mama would remind us.

"Why does he have so many arms?" Sheila would ask.

"To show all of his powers."

"And which god has the elephant face?" I'd ask.

"Ganesh."

"Oh, yeah! I knew that one!" I'd exclaim, my brown curly pigtails bobbing up and down.

Despite the constant questions, Mama never tired of reminding us about other gods, like Shiva, Vishnu, and Shakti.

Mama accepted the absence of her beloved Indian soap operas and looked forward to watching episodes of *Matlock* instead. She tolerated my daily violin practice—even applauded the screeching as I drew my bow across the strings—when she should've been reciting her prayers in absolute silence and with unwavering focus.

A Sari in the Desert

When I told her I could walk to school on my own, Mama ignored me. She'd set down her Hindu prayer book, slide her feet into her worn leather *chappals*, remove her silver hairpin to tidy her bun and repin it, wrap her beige wool shawl around her five-foot frame, lock the front-door deadbolt right below the tilted mezuzah Mom had installed on our doorpost, and wrap her house key in a clean white cotton handkerchief before stuffing it into her bra. Next, she'd grab my seven-year-old hand in her own brown one, worn smooth by years of making traditional whole-wheat chapatis by hand, and say, "We walk to school now."

Juan, Two, Three

TASSIE KALAS HANEY

*W*hen my husband left me for a sexy one-bedroom midtown apartment and a racy two-seater convertible, I wanted revenge.

Nothing would have made me happier than swinging my son's official Little League baseball bat at the contrite expression on his apologetic face. Stuck with a five-bedroom home in the suburbs of Houston, three children under the age of twelve, and a soccer-mom Suburban, I agonized over my broken family and shattered dreams. My future seemed as bright as the shallow-cut half-carat I slipped off my finger and into a dresser drawer.

But what I worried most about being a single mom was that my children would be cheated out of family vacations. It had been hard enough to juggle their daily routines when I was married. Two parents trying to tackle school, homework, and extracurricular activities for three children was challenging—almost impossible if one parent did his share by shouting encouragement from his spot on the sofa in front of the TV.

After my divorce, traveling alone with three children across *town* was daunting enough. Traveling with them out of the country could have proven to be the surest way to give a newly liberated mother a one-way ticket to a nervous breakdown.

But I was freshly divorced and fueled by anger and self-righteousness. I longed for white beaches and tropical drinks and for my children to believe their mom was superwoman disguised in denim shorts and silver bangles. Warm and sunny was what we all needed after a long, dark year.

I went to the travel agency and purchased four tickets to Cancún. Then I checked our passports, flipping them open one by one to make sure none had expired.

I examined my own photo first. Taken when I was still a blissful bride, my hair hung in soft brown waves past my shoulders. My younger self gazed into the camera with an open, unguarded smile. She was a woman who was confident her husband loved her, no matter how unflattering her passport picture might be. A woman who trusted that the future held exotic destinations and happy times ahead.

I opened my son Alston's next. He grinned back at me from the tiny postage-stamp-size photo. Athletic and witty and a little reserved, he already towered over me, and I could always count on my oldest to add teenage humor to any situation.

My middle child's passport was next. Kati, with her curly hair, was serious and smart, always challenging herself to excel, and even at the age of twelve, she was willing to mother the rest of us with her worldly advice.

I opened Kristina's book last and smiled when I saw her wide brown eyes staring back at me from behind a pair of glasses. Thin and delicate, with long brown hair that never seemed brushed, my sensitive but outspoken youngest child worried over our family, like a Greek grandmother in an eight-year-old body.

I hugged the blue-leather passports to my chest and took a deep breath. To me, they symbolized freedom. I was eager to prove to everyone, and myself, that our adventures were just beginning.

I broke the news to my mother first.

"Are you sure?" my mother asked in a worried voice when she found out I was taking her precious grandchildren to a foreign country. "There are drug wars there. Why don't you just borrow the beach house for the week if you want to get away? There's a lot to do in Galveston."

Then I told my ex-husband.

"Do you really think that's a good idea?" he asked, trying his usual passive-aggressive tactics, which no longer had an effect on me. "Don't I have to give you permission to take them out of the country?"

Their lack of confidence in me was the motivation I needed to get us packed and boarded on the plane. When we arrived at our palatial resort and I saw the children's eyes light up as they spotted the pool, I knew I'd made the right decision. What could possibly go wrong?

We wouldn't spend all week by the pool, I vowed. That was a safe, married thing to do. I directed us to the excursion desk. We had to immerse ourselves in the culture and embrace the customs of the country.

"Welcome!" A tan woman with glossy black hair and a pink peasant dress greeted us with a blinding smile. She smelled of sunshine and coconuts. "What a beautiful family. How can I help you?"

One look at her, and I wished I'd packed one of those miracle bathing suits that were guaranteed to make the wearer look ten pounds lighter in ten seconds, instead of my frumpy floral two-piece. I leafed through a colorful binder on her desk. "I'd like to book an excursion for my children and me."

"Of course! I can help you." She looked over my shoulder expectantly. "Should we wait for your husband?"

"Excuse me?" I'd been waiting on him for the last twelve years.

My son stared at her, his mouth hanging open. "She kind of looks like that actress Dad likes on *Modern Family*," he said under his breath.

"She's beautiful," Kristina whispered. Her brown eyes widened. "Like one of my Barbie dolls."

Kati wrinkled her nose.

The woman pursed her pouty lips. "I'd like to talk to both you and your husband," she persisted, her tone growing an edge.

I narrowed my eyes. *And I'm sure he'd like to talk to you.* "Why?" I thrust my chin up in defiance, and it quivered a little. *Tell her. Just admit to Miss Mexico that your husband was the one piece of baggage you left at home. Why can't you say the D-word? D-umped. D-itched. D-ivorced.*

Miss Mexico continued. "I want to let both of you know about the amazing opportunities here to own a condo of your own." She looked annoyed, like a man-less female had never dared approach her desk.

"No husband." I looked her in the eye and dared her to dismiss me. I watched her eyes dull and her chest heave as a huge sigh escaped her lips. "Don't be sad," I said, shrugging and lying just a little. "I'm not."

With a forced smile, she recited a memorized list of the excursions then glanced at her watch. I slapped my Visa into her hand and purchased four tickets to Chichen Itza for the next morning.

Enjoy an unforgettable excursion back into the times of the Mayan empire, the brochure promised. *Ride in comfort in an air-conditioned bus!*

I hesitated. It had been years since I'd ridden a bus. I flashed back to a youth group trip I'd taken as a young girl to Wyoming, when the altitude and winding roads and a cute boy from Dallas made me weak in my knees. But I was stronger now. I'd stomached heartbreak and a hearty helping of humble pie in the past year. A two-hour bus ride would be a piece of tres leches.

Stop for an authentic buffet lunch in a scenic town on the way to one of the Seven Wonders of the World. I smiled. My husband would have hated it.

Perfect.

We spent the afternoon at the hotel beach, swimming in the tranquil turquoise sea. The girls got their hair braided by an old woman selling scarves and trinkets, and the kids and I sipped frozen drinks out of coconuts, mine dosed with a healthy shot of rum. I settled onto a plush chaise lounge and smiled. Wiggling my toes, I watched the fine white sand sift through them and finally felt myself relax. I might have no longer been a good wife, and that wasn't my fault, but I was still a good mother.

The wake-up call came too early the next morning. I dragged the kids out of bed, sprayed them with Coppertone 70, and filled my backpack with essentials for the day. Dramamine for car sickness, snacks and Gatorade—no way we were drinking the water in Mexico—money, and a credit card. When we had boarded the bus on time and settled into the first two rows, I took a deep breath of the stale air and smiled at the children, certain we were prepared for anything. Nothing bad would happen to these kids while Supermom was in charge.

A smooth-talking tour guide with dark wavy hair welcomed us. Juan, a self-professed expert in Mayan history and culture, would accompany us to lunch, lead us through the ruins, and then bring us back to our hotel in time for dinner.

"We have such an exciting, fun day planned." Juan's heavily accented English was amplified through the poor-quality microphone he held. "Unless, of course, you're a virgin." His eyes scanned the bus and settled on a curvy teen sitting next to her mother. "The Mayan priests in the Yucatán sacrificed virgins by throwing them into sinkholes, or cenotes, to petition the gods for rain and fertile fields."

Kati blushed.

"I hope *you're* not a virgin, Mom!" Kristina drew closer to me, her beaded braids pressed against my chest.

Juan's bushy eyebrows danced up and down. "Best *not* to be a virgin for too long in the Mayan culture."

Alston scrunched up his face. "Yuck-atan."

"You'll be happy to know our bus has a restroom." Juan gestured to the back. "But it's a Mexican restroom, not an American one." He paused and waited for us to stop wondering out loud. "This means, if you have to go number one, *no problema*. If you have to go number two . . ." He held his nose and fanned his face. "Raise your hand like this." He raised his arm and made the peace sign with his fingers. "And that will be the signal for me to tell the driver to pull over at the nearest rest stop for you to do your business." His tone grew more serious. "We're not equipped to handle *numero dos*. *Comprende?*"

I gasped. I couldn't imagine what kind of person would actually notify the entire bus that they had to have a bowel movement, much less force everyone to pull over while they did the deed. I rolled my eyes. Only in Mexico!

The kids dozed off during Juan's lecture. He explained that

Chichen Itza meant "the mouth at the well of Itza." The huge area, composed of architectural wonders, contained a temple and an ancient playing field.

After an especially dramatic description of the mystical powers of the pyramids, Juan shut off his microphone and ambled down the aisle, pausing to laugh and joke along the way. He stopped by my seat, glanced at my sleeping children, and then reverted his gaze back to me, allowing it to linger.

"Your husband doesn't want to explore the pyramids?" He flashed a brilliant smile.

"Not these, anyway," I shot back. Then I remembered my children were in hearing range and pressed my lips together grimly.

He raised his eyebrows and stared at me a second too long, then made his way back down the aisle. I cringed at the unwelcome attention. An hour later, we pulled up outside a tired-looking hotel in the middle of nowhere.

"And now let's break for a delicious authentic Yucatán meal." Juan stood by the driver as we exited the bus. "All you can eat!"

I herded the kids together. "Remember, don't drink the water." The last thing we needed on this trip was a family epidemic of Montezuma's revenge.

We walked up to an unimpressive buffet line. The kids examined the selection and hesitantly picked up plates.

"My, oh Maya!" Alston held up a soggy sausage with a pair of tongs. "This looks good."

I slapped the sausage out of his hand. "No pork! I googled it. Undercooked pork is a recipe for disaster. Try rice, beans, or tortillas." I examined each item they put on their plates like an FDA inspector. "No fresh fruit or salad." I speared a piece of chicken with a serving fork and placed it on my plate next to a portion of fish smothered in sauce. "And don't drink the water!"

We sat at a long table, and the kids picked at their food. Too chicken to eat much chicken, I nibbled at the lukewarm fish, changed my mind, and spooned some refried beans into my mouth.

Juan sauntered up to our table and glanced at my half-eaten plate. "Are you enjoying the carnitas?"

"No carnitas for me. Just a little chicken."

"No, mama, that's carnitas." Juan smirked at the expression on my face. "Pork. Mexican style."

I had *thought* it looked a little gray. Trying to keep the worry from my face, I gathered the children up, and we followed the others back onto the bus. Juan played Mariachi music on an eight-track tape player all the way to the ruins. My tummy rumbled to the festive beat.

We filed off the bus and followed Juan to the entrance. He chattered happily, pointing out the information desk and restrooms, and then slowed down to walk by my side.

He tapped my arm to get my attention and pointed to an ambulance parked by the gate. "That's in case someone gets sick." His expression grew ominous, and he continued in a singsong voice. "You never know." A chill ran up my spine despite the hot tropical sun. He nodded, then hurried off to the front of the line to lead our group on a tour of the grounds.

An angry sun glared down directly into my eyes. Humidity weighed heavily on my shoulders, and within minutes I was drenched with sweat. My legs felt heavy, and I seemed to be moving in slow motion as I struggled to keep up with the others.

Alston saw I was lagging behind and slowed down to wait for me. "Hurry up, Mom! We're going to see the Great Ball Court." He allowed me to clutch his arm. "Juan says if you clap at one end of the field, it will produce nine echoes at the center." He felt the clamminess of my hand against his skin and studied my face. "You don't look so good."

"I'm feeling a little dizzy. The heat . . ."

I felt weak. My legs were shaking by the time we made it to the court where Juan was demonstrating how sound carried by clapping his hands sharply while the others listened half a football field away. I clung onto Alston for support, waiting for Juan to finish his explanation so I could ask him where I could find a spot to sit in the shade until I felt better. My stomach bloated over my waistband, and I undid the button of my jeans.

Juan clapped again for the group, and they clapped back nine times in response, in awe of the acoustics of the court. He noticed me standing beside him in the silent moment that followed, and his eyes lit up. I could smell his aftershave as he leaned in to whisper something in my ear. Before the first flirtatious comment could escape his lips, my body made a noise of its own, sending him reeling away in disgust.

"Mom!" Alston's mouth hung open in teenage admiration.

The explosive clap from my bowels ripped across the court, nine sharp blasts resonating in the middle where the tour group huddled. They laughed and cheered in response, then blew nine ripe raspberries back at us.

Juan glared at me. Seconds away from having the runs at the ruins, I clutched my stomach and hobbled, doubled over, to the restroom by the entrance. Agonizing cramps seared through my body as I waited in line to use the tiny facilities. I contemplated finding the closest sinkhole and sacrificing myself to the gods, but given my marital history, I was sure I'd be spewed out in exchange for the nearest virgin.

As I inched my way closer to the front, I realized with horror that an old woman dressed all in black was rationing out squares of toilet paper. One, two, three squares—each woman in line was allocated the same amount. When I reached her, she distributed three sheets of the rough, thin tissue to me, took one look at my sweaty face, and handed me one more. I stayed holed up in the steamy stall until Kati and Kristina wandered in an hour later, frantically calling my name.

Somehow, they loaded me onto the bus and sat me in the aisle seat next to Kristina. "I wish Dad were here," she whimpered. She fanned me with a map of Chichen Itza while Kati gave me small sips of water from a bottle.

For an agonizing hour, I concentrated on clenching, begging my bowels to respect the rules of the bus and remain calm on the long trip to the resort. Somehow, I made it halfway back to Cancún. Then, without warning and without raising my hand, I leaped from my seat and sprinted down the aisle to the back of the bus. I did number one and number two and what must have been number three in the tiny restroom, fearing the whole time how the Mexican plumbing would react to my insubordination.

No Juan must know!

I considered my options. If I extended my stay in the steamy potty, it would raise suspicion. But if I exited, I feared what repercussions awaited me on the other side of the door.

I slapped cold water on my face, gearing up for my walk of shame. I'd traumatized my children and made a mess of this trip, this tour, and my life. The least I could have done was raise my hand to warn the innocent bystanders.

I cracked open the door, expecting to find a sea of Shit-chen Itza flowing down the aisle. But miraculously, the floor was bare. A few passengers had even managed to sleep through my eruption. Juan stared at me warily as I returned to my seat and collapsed beside Kristina. I knew I could count on my youngest for sympathy and a loving hand to hold.

She took one look at me and edged closer to the window. "You look green." She shuddered. "And you smell funny."

I mustered up the last of my strength to scavenge through my backpack and dug out a half-filled lukewarm Gatorade. I took a few tiny sips of the tepid liquid and cradled the bottle all the way back to the hotel.

When the bus jerked to a stop outside our hotel, I was the first out the door, my kids following close behind me. So thankful to be off the bumpy bus and near a real working toilet, I almost kissed the ground. I shoved some crumpled bills into the tour guide's outstretched palm.

Juan shook my hand and held it a moment too long. "Tell your husband he missed out."

I stared back at him. "He already knows."

Then the bus ride, the undercooked pork, and the past year of my life gurgled out of my stomach and up my throat, and I raced through the lobby to the ladies' room.

Miss Mexico found me hugging the toilet, my cheek pressed against the cool porcelain.

"I gave your children some ice cream." She handed me a wet paper towel under the stall door.

"Thanks," I mumbled weakly and unlocked the door. I joined her in front of the mirrors and examined my disheveled appearance. Mascara ran down my face, and the front of my shirt was stained with something the color of refried beans. In comparison, Miss Mexico looked like she was seconds away from accepting her crown.

She reached into her roomy handbag and pulled out a shot glass. "This is for you."

I shook my head. Alcohol was the last thing I needed. What was wrong with this crazy lady? And what was wrong with me for thinking I could do this alone?

She pulled out a shaker of salt and a lime wedge and placed them on the sink.

The thought of tequila almost sent me reeling back to the stall. "Thanks, but no thanks. Really."

She reached in a third time and pulled out a bottle of Imodium and waved it in the air. "Ancient Mexican remedy." She poured a long shot into the tiny glass. "From Wal-Mart." Then she sprinkled my palm with salt. She waited while I licked my hand, swallowed the shot, and sucked on the tart wedge of lime.

I felt better.

"Not many women are brave enough to travel alone with their children." She nodded her head at my reflection. "But you're giving them the gift of seeing the world."

I smiled feebly.

"Sometimes it's an imperfect world, no? But they'll always remember you traveled it together."

I really felt better now. Miss Mexico's acceptance speech was just the cure I needed.

I looked at the younger woman with new eyes. "How'd you get so wise?"

Her lips curled into a sad smile. "You're not the only person who's ever had a broken heart."

We walked back out into the lobby together. The children were huddled around the excursion desk, half-eaten ice cream cones in their hands, poring over the daily tour binder. My heart swelled at the sight of them. In that instant, I realized I may no longer be married, but this handful of happily ever after was all mine. Until death do us part.

"Look, Mom!" Kati pointed to a picture of a tropical paradise. "Visit Xel-Há aquatic theme park!" she read. "Satisfy your appetite for family fun and adventure. Snorkeling, zip-lining, and all you can eat at our international buffet."

I looked at Miss Mexico with alarm.

"Don't worry," my new friend said. "We can pack you a lunch. And it's a short taxi ride away."

I raised one hand in the air, two fingers making the victory sign, slapped my Visa into her outstretched palm with the other, and hurried back to the bathroom. I still wasn't 100 percent, but I was getting there. In the meantime, there was a whole world to explore, and I wouldn't settle for just any Juan along the way. My kids had bounced back, and so would I.

And that was the greatest revenge of all.

Milwaukee

Sage Webb

*M*aybe different cities have different kinds of cold. Or maybe places in general have different colds. When the bus stopped in Chicago, the driver opened the door and cold swept in, but it wasn't like the cold we'd left in Michigan, and it wasn't like the cold of a Marshals lockup. Chicago cold had sharper edges. Cold in Michigan was worn out, with rounded corners, used up and yielding. And cold in a lockup is its own thing.

The hurt of the Chicago cold made me resent Jacob.

"It's fuckin' freezing, man," I shouted to him over the voices of two women on cell phones calling their people for rides from the bus station.

"It ain't so bad." Jacob had read a self-help book a couple of years ago and became a this-ain't-so-bad type of person.

"Do you know where the fuck we're going? Let's find a bus to Milwaukee." I stopped in front of the door to the station, scanning the placards of the buses at the curb.

"I ain't gettin' on no more buses today." Jacob's breath puffed in front of his lips, and we were both shouting a little because of the wind and the general noise of travel, of people going somewhere else.

"Well, I ain't wanderin' around this city in this fuckin' cold, man."

I shoved my hands in the pockets of my jacket. It was an old jacket and made for fall, not winter—and we were beyond fall cold.

"We'll play some music. Then maybe we can get a decent dinner." Jacob took a few steps and rounded the corner of the bus station, and I followed him because I didn't want to argue and I wasn't much in the mood for another bus ride either.

The sun felt weak and like it didn't want to crawl past the buildings to the concrete and dirty puddles and gum stains on the sidewalks, and as we walked across the river and past the city's Chipotles and Burger Kings, I shivered. Jacob stopped on a corner next to a big Macy's and said we could set up and play there, and I resented him even more.

"I ain't playin' here. It's fuckin' cold, man. Plus, you probably need a license or something to play on the street. I don't want to deal with that bullshit."

"Shut up already about the cold." He pulled a Martin Backpacker out of his bag. It had been in the trunk when we'd gotten arrested on I-94.

I dug in my backpack for a harmonica. My lips had cracked, and my hands felt too heavy to play. "I can't, man. Let's just go find a bus and go home. This is fuckin' crazy."

"Where you want to go?" Jacob fiddled with the guitar's tuning pegs.

"I don't know. Not here." I hunched my shoulders and turned my back to the wind.

"Houston?" He stopped working on the strings and looked at me. I stared back at him.

"Corpus?" He strummed the guitar and made another adjustment. "Aw, fuck no. I ain't goin' back there."

He leaned down and pulled a capo out of the bag he'd dropped at his feet. Neither of us spoke again until he launched into "Wagon Wheel" and he started singing to people walking past about his plan to head down south, to the land of the pines, and thumb his way to North Caroline. Toward the end of the song, a kid stopped in front of me. He looked about eight years old.

"Come on, honey." The woman with him pulled on his arm.

The kid kept standing there, watching us. He smiled, and the woman pulled again.

"Honey, come on."

She picked the boy up. He watched me over her shoulder as she walked away.

A woman in a long down coat stopped in front of us. "What a bitch," this new woman said to no one, and it didn't make much sense, really. She laughed then, loudly, and stood watching me and Jacob, and I started feeling uncomfortable.

"Let's go," I said to Jacob.

The new woman heard me.

"No," she said, shouting a little to reach above the wind. "Stay—I like your music."

Jacob kept singing, and I tried to ignore the chick, put my instrument to my chapped lips, and blew hard.

"I got a dollar," she said. She dug in a pocket, making an exaggerated show of it. She put a five-dollar bill in Jacob's bag, which he'd arranged in front of his feet, unzipped and seeded with two one-dollar bills.

The woman's eyes wandered, and she swayed and bounced out of time with our rhythm. After a while, she removed a phone from a pocket and began texting into it. After another while, a man in a pink button-down shirt and Sperry boat shoes walked up to the woman. He wore an unzipped North Face jacket over the pink shirt. He looked like a guy I'd worked with, a dude who spent everything he made on clothes and jewelry and shit like that and ended up testifying against me at trial.

"What you up to, baby girl?" the dude asked the woman.

"Hey!" she shouted back. "I'm listening to music."

"Come on. Let's bounce." The guy nodded up the street.

"Uh-uh," the woman said. She shook her head, and then she kept shaking it, and her hair fell over her face, and she shut her eyes.

"Give 'em a buck," she said after a bit. "They're good."

"Nah, come on," the man said again.

"Fine." The chick raised her head and brushed the hair out of her eyes and stopped acting the fool. "Where'd you want to go?" She held back and didn't start walking with the man.

"Wherever. I don't care. Let's get something to eat."

"Okay, but give these dudes something. They're cool." She gestured to Jacob's bag.

"I got no cash," the man said.

"Fuck you. You got cash." She pulled her arm away from the man.

The guy unzipped a pocket of the jacket and took out a wallet. He pulled two one-dollar bills from it and held them out to her. She took the money and stepped over to Jacob's bag and set the bills in it.

Jacob nodded at her. She smiled, the dude stared into his phone, and I thought back to the days when these two fools would have been potential customers. I knew them: the privilege, the self-indulgence, the boredom. College kids with tuition-paying parents and a taste for whatever it was the products I once imported gave people who already had everything they needed. When Jacob stopped singing, I put my harmonica in my pocket.

"Let's go," I said. "We got enough."

"Naw, a couple more," Jacob said. "There's people out."

"Naw, fuck that. We got nine bucks. I'm hungry. Let's go to McDonald's."

I reached down and plucked the bills from Jacob's bag. Behind me, the woman sounded shrill when she shouted.

"You hungry? Why don't you come with us? My boyfriend, he's hungry."

"Aw, hell no." The guy looked up from his phone. He knew I could do nothing for him, had nothing to offer him. Louder, he said, "Sorry, man, no disrespect, but we gotta bounce." He took hold of the woman again.

"No, come on. We got nowhere to go. Let's meet these dudes." The woman pulled her arm away. "Come on," she said to me, "we'll buy you dinner. Where you from?"

"Texas," Jacob said. "But we been in Michigan the last couple years."

I'd had enough nonsense. "FCI Milan," I said.

"What's that?" the woman asked.

"It's a federal facility," Jacob said.

"Like a nuthouse?" She cocked her head.

"Like a prison," I said.

"That's cool." She grinned.

"Not really." I tried to catch Jacob's eye.

"Well, we'll buy you dinner," she said. "You want the Signature Room?"

The boyfriend stepped up. "We're not going to the Signature Room with these guys. Come on." Again, the pull on the arm, this one harder. The girl took a step toward the dude.

"Sorry, man. No disrespect," the guy repeated, "but she just does this shit to piss off her mom. Peace." He hitched two fingers toward me in some sort of salute.

People do a lot of things to piss off their moms. That shit used to be profitable, but I was done with all of it now, even free dinners.

"Let's get something to eat," I said to Jacob.

"With us," the girl called, pulling away from the boyfriend and returning to us, pushing the strap of a large purse back up her arm onto her shoulder. "The Signature Room."

"Sure, whatever. You're paying?" Jacob looked at her. His self-help book hadn't fixed his mindset.

"Yeah." The crazy bitch pulled two one-hundred-dollar bills out of a coat pocket and held them out. "Right here."

Jacob shrugged, picked up his bag, and shoved his guitar into it.

We followed the couple, and I watched Jacob's bag bang against his back, until the chick turned a corner to lead us into a dark building with a revolving door that made me feel weird, like it was spinning me from the windchill and noise of the street into too much emptiness and quiet. The boyfriend, who hadn't said anything while we were walking, tilted his head toward some elevators. My ears popped as we stood in the box that dragged us upward, and we all looked away from one another because we knew we didn't belong in that box together.

We didn't belong at the host stand either, and the dude at the stand looked at us when the chick asked for a table by a window. The boyfriend walked off toward the sign for the restroom.

"It's cool," the girl said to the host. "They're cool. Here, put us by the window, and here." She held out one of her one-hundred-dollar bills.

We followed the dude to a table, and Jacob pulled out the chair by the aisle, so I had to take the seat by the window. I looked down toward the big lake a thousand feet below, and my stomach and throat felt weird. I remembered that feeling from somewhere else, maybe my sentencing hearing or something. After we sat down, the girl got right back up.

"I gotta pee. I'll be right back. If Nick comes back, tell him to get me some wine. Red."

"Sure," Jacob said.

I waited for her to make it past the host stand and the elevators and then stood up. "Let's get the fuck out of here. This is some fucked-up shit."

"You serious? No way. I'm eating a nice dinner on this bitch's dime." Jacob opened a menu.

"Seriously? That's a crazy bitch."

"Sit down," Jacob said. "The dude's coming over here."

The boyfriend, Nick, walked toward the table. I sat down. When Nick arrived at the table, he sat across from Jacob. His eyes seemed too wide. He opened a menu and held it close to his face.

"Your girlfriend told us to ask you to get her some red wine," Jacob said to him. "She went to pee."

"Sure," Nick said. "Wine. Yeah, let's get some wine."

He set his menu down and groped for the wine list, lifting and dropping the woman's menu and my menu in his search. When he picked up the list, which had been sitting by his right elbow, he looked at it like broke-ass guys look at eight balls.

"Look here, gentlemen," he said after a while. "A Cabernet Sauvignon from Shafer Vineyards: One Point Five. From Napa. I like Napa. 2014—a good year. Only $180; we'll get two bottles for the table. You ever been to Napa?"

He turned to me. Jacob hunched behind his menu.

"No," I answered.

"It's a nice place. I went there a couple years ago for a buddy's bachelor party. Got so wasted. What do you want to eat? How about the lamb chops? Or a steak? I think I'm going to have the surf and turf. We should all have the surf and turf—except Leslie won't have the surf and turf. She's a vegetarian. Pescatarian, actually. She'll have the surf, just not the turf. So she won't get surf and turf. I'll get her the scallops. So surf and turf for everyone else?"

"Sure," Jacob said. He shut his menu and put it on the plain white plate in front of him.

I shrugged.

When a waiter approached us, Nick got a little louder. He ordered the wine.

"And let's do a mushroom strudel to start. Sound good?" He looked from me to Jacob.

"All right," Jacob said.

The waiter walked off. Below us, the lake had turned the color of concertina wire with the sun setting on the other side of the building. I was looking at it when the woman—Leslie—returned. She pulled out the chair across from me. She still had her coat on, and I tried to keep my eyes on the lake as she struggled out of it.

"We've decided on surf and turf for the table and scallops for you," Nick said. "I ordered cab for the table."

"That's fine. It's pretty out, huh? You know, I'll text Megan. She should meet us here. I'll bet she's around. She should come have a drink with us. Meet our new friends. Don't you think? I'll text her."

Leslie twisted around, mumbling and leaning over the back of her chair.

"Megan's laid up, remember?" Nick rolled his eyes.

Leslie untwisted, phone in hand, and Nick faced her and the window. I was glad I was outside their conversation.

"She went in for her abortion today, remember?" Nick snorted. "She won't be around for days. I'm sure of it."

"Oh, yeah. I forgot. Maybe I should text her." Leslie looked like she was talking to the tablecloth. "I'll see if she's all right." She stared into her phone, swaying a little as she started punching her finger into the screen.

"Text her later, boo. You're being rude."

"Just lemme text her really quick." She finished with the phone and set it next to her plate. The screen reflected off the dark window. "What're your names?" She turned to look at me and Jacob and set her elbows on either side of the plate and silverware in front of her and set her chin in her hands.

"I'm Jacob. This is Neil."

"And you're from Texas?"

"Yeah, Corpus Christi," Jacob answered.

"But you were in prison?"

"For a while," Jacob said.

"Where are you going now? What brought you to Chicago?"

"We're going to Milwaukee." Jacob dug a nail into the hollow behind his right ear.

The waiter returned, held a bottle of wine out to Nick. Nick looked at the label. I watched the cars way below us. After he'd finished pouring wine into our glasses, the waiter looked at me and Jacob for too long. I turned away from the window and caught him at it, and he looked away.

"Why are you going to Milwaukee?" Leslie asked.

"Friend of ours has jobs for us there," Jacob answered.

"Well, that's perfect! We go to school in Madison," Leslie said. "We're just chilling at my mom's place this weekend. She's on a photo safari in Africa. Where'd she go again?" She turned to Nick and grabbed his arm. "Where'd she go? The name of the country? That my mom's in." She glanced at me. "He knows. He's good with remembering stuff like that." She shifted back to him. "Where'd she go, Nick?"

"Kenya. She's in Kenya, boo." Nick rolled his eyes again, took a long sip of wine.

I hadn't touched my glass yet. I reached for it.

"It's good, huh?" Leslie looked at me and nodded her head fast.

"Sure."

The wine violated my supervised release, but I had two more days before I had to report to the probation office.

"You can stay with us if you want. At my mom's place. We'll drive you to Milwaukee on our way back to Madison tomorrow. My mom has a nice place. You can stay there. Are you guys allergic to cats? She has two cats. Nick hates cats, but he says these are okay because they don't come out much. And they don't shed much. And they're hypoallergenic. So even if you're allergic, you should be okay. It's just for the night too. Right? It should be fine."

"Sure," Jacob said. "We're fine with cats."

The lights in the buildings around and below us were coming on, little gold squares strung across the city.

The waiter came back with the mushroom appetizer, and Nick ordered the rest of the food. The waiter poured more wine into all the glasses before he walked away. He didn't look at me. Leslie started talking about music, asked something about music, and Jacob said something to her.

Nick shook his head. "She listens to Justin Timberlake." He picked up one of the wine bottles, grinned, and took a long swig from it. His eyes had turned that familiar red. He put the bottle down, rested his forearms on the table, and leaned over toward me, forcing Leslie to sit back in her chair.

"So you guys were in prison? What for?"

"Murder," Jacob said. "Killing a couple motherfuckers."

"I thought you said it was federal. What'd you do? Kill some Indian motherfucker on a reservation?" He laughed. "My dad's an attorney. You didn't kill anyone."

He looked at me again, and below us, pocks of red spread down the lakeshore as traffic backed up.

"Cocaine," Jacob said. "A lot of cocaine. And all the shit that goes with it."

"Shit? Like what shit?"

"Like firearms in furtherance of, maintaining a drug house, supps for priors. Let's see. What else, Neil?" I didn't look up. Jacob kept running his mouth. "We went to trial, so it was a lot. The government interceded a couple a times. There were a bunch of counts."

The truth was he remembered every word of each of the indictments, every page, every charge. I knew he did. I remembered.

"How'd they catch you?"

"They pulled me over for an obstructed license plate on 94 outside Battle Creek. We were bringing a bunch of shit up from the border. Somebody dropped a dime."

"How long'd you get?"

The waiter and another guy arrived with the food. The other guy stood in the background as the waiter set plates in front of us and asked how everything looked. Jacob never answered about sentencing. He took a bite of steak right away and chewed for a long time. And then we all just ate for a while.

Leslie bobbed her head as she chewed. Nick put the empty wine bottles at the edge of the table, and the waiter took them away. Nick ordered old-fashioneds for the table.

"I gotta piss," he said after the waiter left. "Be right back."

"Do you like the food?" Leslie asked.

"Sure, it's good. Best we've had in a while," Jacob said. He was chewing and grinning and had gone even further up the it-ain't-so-bad scale.

"You want to try a scallop?" Leslie speared a scallop and held it across the table on her fork. Jacob shifted in his seat. He looked at me; I turned away.

"Here," she said, poking the fork toward him. "Just try it. It's fine. Take it." She circled the fork. "I don't bite. I like you."

Jacob glanced at me again, ran a hand through his hair. Then he sighed, and I felt him lean forward. I kept looking out the window, but I sensed him eat that scallop off her fork.

"I'm missing the party, huh?" Nick took his seat again. He spread his napkin in his lap and looked toward me. The waiter appeared with the new drinks.

"So were you like someone's bitch in prison?" Neil took his time lifting the liquor to his mouth.

"Shut the fuck up, Nick," Leslie said. "What the fuck is wrong with you?"

"It's no big thing. It happens to everybody in there." He watched me over the rim of the glass.

"No," I lied, turning from the lobster in front of me. "To be someone's bitch, I'd a had to look more like you."

Leslie snorted.

"Fuck you." Nick gave up the act with the drink and the glass.

"He's high. And he's pure cancer when he's high. Fuck him. Do you want a scallop?" Leslie held the fleshy circle out to me on her fork.

"No," I said. She put the thing back down on her plate.

"Nick, you're an asshole," she said. She picked up her phone and swiped across the screen. Nick picked up her old-fashioned and drank it.

"Look," she said. "Megan texted me back. She says she feels like shit."

"I'm sure she does," Nick said. "But she'll be ready for another trip to the Eiffel Tower in a couple days."

"Let's go. You're poison," she said. She looked out over the restaurant and must have seen the waiter. She waved.

The guy approached our table, she asked for the check, and when the dude returned, she handed him a credit card.

"My mom's," she said. She leaned toward me. "She's gonna love this."

On the street a thousand feet below the restaurant, she took hold of Jacob's arm.

"We're not far from my mom's place. It's just inland a couple blocks and like half a mile north."

The building was four stories tall and sat behind a black iron gate. When I looked up as Leslie jiggled the gate open, I knew which windows belonged to her mom's place: on the third floor, light shone into the night through glass that wore bat decals and grinning fake skeletons. The windows of a woman who'd have a daughter like this one, a daughter who would have bought from the person I'd been years ago. Standing on that street, looking up and through those windows, I remembered before, remembered selling. And then I remembered taking my boy out in a Spiderman costume— remembered that today was the day before Halloween. I shivered. Maybe it had gotten colder.

We rode to the third floor, and Leslie unlocked the condo. She fiddled with a security box to the right of the door. When I was a kid, I was good with those boxes, which later earned me some criminal-history points. A large gray cat walked up and sat in front of us and began crying.

"Robinette has anxiety issues," Leslie said. "Hang on a sec."

She turned down a hallway, and we heard her shout, "Fucking Graciella. Look at these litter boxes."

Overhead, plastic bats and skeletons and witches on brooms with weird plastic bristles bobbed. They must have been strung up with elastic thread because they bounced up and down when the dude, Nick, walked through the mess to drop onto a pink couch. He sat back and pulled a joint out of a pocket.

"Either of you got a light?" He looked at me and Jacob. "Boo," he shouted. "You got a light somewhere in here?"

Leslie returned from wherever she'd gone, wherever the dirty litter boxes were, with a gray vest-type thing that she put on the squirming, howling cat. She velcroed the vest thing around the animal.

"It's her ThunderShirt," she said. She looked up at us from her knees. The cat had stopped wiggling and had flopped down next to her. "It helps with her anxiety. She has a lot of anxiety issues. And she was here alone all day. Poor Miss Robinette. It's gotten worse as she's gotten older."

"Where's a light, babe?" Nick lay across the sofa, flipping the joint back and forth between his fingers.

"I'm busy with the cat. I'll get it in a second. There's gotta be one in the kitchen. You go get it. Look in the drawer by the stove."

She stayed on the floor, petting the cat. It lay on the carpet, panting. "Take off your shoes, would you?" She kept looking at the cat, but she pointed to a wooden shelf by the door behind Jacob. A pair of high heels sat on it. They looked like they were made of black-and-white snake skin.

"Boo, you done with that cat? Get me the lighter, okay?"

I looked at Jacob. I thought about backing out the door. We could find a shelter. I wanted nothing from these people. They—the big "they," the "them" of all "these people"—had taken enough from me, just like I'd taken from them. We were square now and I was done with them. But Jacob had bent and was untying a shoe. Another cat came around a corner and rubbed against the shoe. Nick got off the couch and walked down a hall.

"You guys can sleep in the spare salon." Leslie looked up from the gray cat, the one in the shirt, and pointed down a different hallway. "One of you can sleep in there, and then it adjoins a guest room. There are a bunch of blankets and sheets in the closet in the guest room. It's right down there. Third door on the right. You go check it out. And then we can get something to drink. You can play us some music. I'll stay here with Miss Robinette."

She picked the cat up and held it like a baby. It didn't make any noise with the shirt on. Jacob turned to me, shrugged, and started down the hallway Leslie had pointed toward. I put my shoes on the shelf and followed him. The hallway had paperboard gravestones on the walls, and cloth ghosts hung by their necks from the ceiling.

The guest space was all pink and red, kind of like the couch Nick had been on. The bedroom area had a big covered bed, like something from an old castle. The area next to it had a living room and then a kitchen area. It was like a separate apartment in the condo. It didn't have any of the freaky decorations in it, but it still felt fake, the way the ghosts in the hall were fake. Jacob sat down on the bed.

"Let's get the fuck outta here," I said to him. "This is fucking weird. That chick is fucked in the head and the dude's an asshole, and I'm done with these fools."

"You want to sleep here or at some mission?

"A mission."

Jacob laid back on the bed. "It's nice."

"Yeah, so's not getting arrested for weed, crack, and whatever else that crazy motherfucker's got on him. I don't need these people. I don't want anything from these people. I want to bounce."

"Fuckin' relax. It's warm in here. We got a real place to sleep. We'll leave early and get a bus. Kevin'll pick us up when we get in and everything'll be fine. See what's in that closet." Jacob pointed to the closet doors.

I found a red comforter with gold horse heads on it, two red pillows, and a vibrator under a stack of sheets.

"Bitch's got bedding and a dildo in here." I snorted. "Or maybe it's Megan's." I was surprised I remembered the friend's name, and then I was surprised that I kind of chuckled.

"What the fuck is wrong with you, man?" Jacob sat up. He laughed too. "Chill. Just get your blankets and go sleep on that couch."

"You want something to drink?" Leslie stood in the doorway to the guest room. She had a bottle of vodka in one hand and a bag of weed in the other. "Nick wants to party." She held up the weed. "This stuff isn't bad. I got it from a guy from Kenosha."

"Nah, thanks, I'm good." I stood in front of the closet, holding the horse comforter and pillows.

"Sure. What else ya got?" Jacob pushed himself off the bed and walked over to her.

"Come see." She walked off down the hall.

I shook my head. "Dude, you gotta drop in two days."

Jacob shrugged.

"Whatever." I walked past him to the guest living room and put the pillows and comforter on the couch. I didn't take off my clothes.

We got up around four in the morning. Jacob's eyes were deep red. We got our shoes off the shelf by the door and walked out the black iron gate and found our way down to Randolph Street. I remembered it from the day before.

"We need to go that way." I flipped my head to the right, and Jacob followed me.

We crossed the river in the dark on the old metal bridge, and I stopped in the middle. The water was black and silent and (I was sure) very, very cold. Cold like the rest of Chicago. Cold like so many things.

For most of the ride to Milwaukee, I slept, talking myself into relaxing—Leslie and Nick and their funhouse behind us, the scales balanced, the tab square. I'd paid in years, many years, for what that world said I'd taken.

Now I could say I'd done more than look in the window. I'd stepped through the door, even slept in that world for a few hours: the world of mothers on African safaris and $180 wine and condos strung with safety nets I'd never had. It still felt like they'd offered it all to me—the things I'd supposedly taken, the money and the innocence. They'd offered it all for the products I'd traded them. It didn't feel like I'd cheated anyone, but that was the court's call. All I knew now was I didn't want anything from them. I'd seen it and it wasn't worth it . . . unless Kevin failed to come through with the jobs in Milwaukee.

Love and Murder in Tokyo

SHANE HEALY

*C*ourtney never forgot the day her husband died. Marcus was grilling dinner, lemon-sprinkled salmon with a side of sweet potatoes and puffy French bread. Then he collapsed, and the next moment he was writhing on the kitchen tiles. That was the image that stuck with her. Her husband, so handsome and dorky and kindhearted, spasming on the floor.

She called for an ambulance, but there was nothing that could be done. All her skills were useless. She couldn't jump in front of a bullet. There were no snipers to shoot, no bombs to defuse. Brain aneurysms were silent killers. Rare and commonly asymptomatic. The ambulance arrived, unloading calm, serious professionals who rushed Marcus to the hospital, and Courtney stayed with him for the rest of the day, watching helplessly while her best friend died.

It was an ugly death. Not as gruesome as some of the things she'd seen in Afghanistan or Somalia, but ugly. And just like that, her perfect life was ruined.

Everything was a gray blur afterward, like all the color and playfulness had been drained from her universe. There was a funeral. There were phone calls—so many phone calls that she left her cell phone in the upstairs bedroom and didn't check it for three days. Late at night, she started drinking vodka and bourbon that burned her throat.

But there was a surreal element to all of it. Sometimes, she felt so numb that it was like she was drifting inside another woman's dream, not even a nightmare. She was simply hollow, like a plastic mannequin pretending to be alive.

It seemed impossible to Courtney that reality could be so banal and tragic. Last year, she had walked through a park holding Marcus by the hand. They had wondered together how many children they should have and whether the first baby would be a boy or a girl, and they had debated how to raise their kids. Now when she looked at her bank account, she saw all the money they had saved up for a family that would never exist, and it devastated her down to the core. She felt cold, empty, and lonely, desperately wishing for one last conversation with her husband. Her dearest friend.

It got so bad that Courtney refused to leave the house. She was slipping back into the same tired, antisocial habits of her career from before Marcus, sleepwalking through the ruins of her shattered universe. There was a fracture inside her heart, as though two continental plates had slid apart, leaving behind a dark, mutilated abyss. The love inside her had broken into pain and resentment, some kind of blind, directionless hatred for this unfair world.

Contradictory desires tormented her. Sometimes she was seized by self-loathing and wanted to suffer. Other days, she daydreamed of bleak, twisted fantasies in which she bombed cities, kidnapped politicians, and brought down the stale bureaucratic institutions of the modern age. Courtney knew exactly how to inflict pain on the rest of the world and force other people to share her misery.

Courtney wanted to be self-destructive. So she did the dumbest thing she could think of. She called her old boss.

He picked up on the third ring.

"I want back in," said Courtney.

"Aren't you retired?" asked Franklin. He was pretending to be disinterested, but she knew he was excited.

"I need action," she said. "How fast can you get me back in a war zone?"

"What about next week?"

"Tomorrow is better," answered Courtney.

Franklin chuckled. "All right. Pack your suitcases. Tomorrow you're flying to Japan."

"Japan? What about Pakistan?" Courtney argued furiously. "You need me in the field. I should be calling in airstrikes!"

"You're more useful to the bureau in Japan," Franklin said sternly. "Fighting in the Middle East is a lost cause. I refuse to waste another of my best operatives on that meat grinder."

Courtney spent the long flight to Asia reading. For a couple of hours, she thumbed through a Japanese-English dictionary, studying the strange, intricate calligraphy and practicing unfamiliar pronunciations. The words slid awkwardly from her tongue. But she was less rusty than she'd expected. Her ability to learn and retain languages had always been remarkable.

Quickly, Courtney skimmed through a basic travel book to brush up on Japanese customs, protocols, and expectations for foreigners' behavior. Then she put her research to a more difficult test and began to consume modern literature. It was a struggle. Bravely, she plunged into the most famous works of Yukio Mishima, Ryu Murakami, and Shusaku Endo. Each time she finished a chapter, she felt like she'd climbed a mountain. These were difficult passages, even for a native Japanese reader.

She buried herself in linguistics because it was better than reflecting on everything else. Her life was a wreck, and her mission was a mystery. What made Japan special? She couldn't figure out why the CIA cared about the island. Japan had organized crime, but so did America and every other country. Maybe her handlers were concerned about nuclear terrorism. It was definitely a puzzle. Their angle wasn't obvious.

But the more she considered it, the less she cared. What difference would it make whether she was supposed to blackmail, murder, sabotage, steal secrets, or seduce some corrupt world leader? These crimes meant nothing to her. She'd done them all before, and she would do them all again. This mission would distract her from her grief. Courtney just wanted to get away from America, away from all the once-treasured memories of Marcus that were now painful and bittersweet, to escape the sympathetic looks from everyone she knew.

In a city like Tokyo, it was possible for a foreigner to create a new identity. Here, she could be more than just a lonely widow.

She met her handler in the Tokyo airport. He ferried her to a hotel.

"You're very beautiful," leered her supervisor. Courtney found it difficult to believe he'd ever met the rigorous physical standards of the agency. The man was grotesquely obese. Even sitting on the other side of the bed, she could smell the putrid stench of his sweat. He looked like a gross bearded caveman stuffed roughly into an elegant suit, and his black hair was damp and greasy.

"Thanks," she said. They were speaking in Japanese to help her practice. "Let's skip to the briefing. After thirteen hours of cramped travel, I need a little rest."

"Fair enough." Her handler nodded but looked disappointed. Courtney guessed he was accustomed to sleeping with agents. "Your task is straightforward. Japan is a prosperous nation. Factories, skyscrapers, and some of the world's most prestigious hospitals can all be found in Tokyo. Normally that's wonderful. But recently, our agency has learned this island is functioning as a safe haven for terrorists and contract killers. They travel to Japan for medical operations. If enemies of our government want a new face, there's a doctor in Tokyo who provides them with plastic surgery. He's become wealthy by disguising foreign outlaws. Very identifiable terrorists can become anonymous overnight."

Courtney grinned. Suddenly, her assignment had become intriguing. "Who's the surgeon?" she asked.

"Your job is to find out," said the fat man.

Courtney strutted in front of the mirror. She looked sexy. There were a lot of downsides to being a spy, but this was one of the perks—the operational budget to splurge on fabulous clothes. Right now, the agent wore a tight floral dress the same shade of pink as a cherry blossom. It was low-cut and flaunted her curves. She was the embodiment of American beauty: a short, slim blonde with a full figure and, at thirty-five years old, still young. Courtney's goal was to look enticing, and she did.

Courtney left the hotel room and took a taxi to the Suwaru Medical Center.

Yesterday, the obese handler had presented her with a list of three names. Each of the three surgeons was a pioneer in the medical field, brilliant, and extravagantly wealthy. Any one of these men could be her target. They all possessed substantial ambition, resources, and surgical talent, as well as a global network of contacts. But the investigation needed to remain subtle and undetected. Japan was an important American ally. Assassinating or kidnapping one of the country's best doctors would cause a massive political scandal.

Stepping out of the taxi, Courtney strode into the hospital. Her high heels clipped the marble floor with a satisfying firmness, and men turned to stare. On the ninth floor, she entered the office of Dr. Watashi Shokan.

There was a single receptionist sitting behind the counter. The secretary was thin and unattractive.

"Good morning," said Courtney. Her voice was falsely upbeat. "My name is Danielle Schultz, reporter with the Stanford Medical Journal. I have an appointment scheduled to interview Dr. Shokan."

"I thought you were Japanese when we chatted on the phone!" exclaimed the astonished receptionist. Happily, she clapped her hands together. "That's amazing. You don't have an accent at all. And you're so pretty."

"How sweet of you." Courtney smiled, and this time her positivity was authentic. The secretary made a phone call.

Dr. Watashi Shokan emerged from the doorway a few minutes later. Much to Courtney's surprise, he looked like a movie star. Tall and handsome, the surgeon swept into the lobby with the presence of a hurricane, exuding confidence and purposefulness with every movement. Immediately, he was the center of the room, grinning with perfect white teeth. Firmly, the surgeon shook the agent's hand, and she felt the strength of his grip and admired his muscular physique.

Instantly, Courtney disliked Dr. Shokan. Something about his cocky, self-assured swagger reminded her too much of Marcus.

"Where's her translator?" asked the surgeon, turning to his subordinate.

"I speak enough Japanese to manage on my own," said Courtney.

"Excellent," replied Dr. Shokan. He sized her up with a newfound respect. "Please, let's speak in my office."

Together they walked, discussing recent developments in medical innovation while the surgeon led her deep into a sterile labyrinth of corridors, offices, and operating rooms. There was a suspicious number of security cameras.

Courtney focused on saying as little as possible. Every time the conversation steered toward unfamiliar territory, she pivoted, asking Dr. Shokan's opinion about some other topic. He was an amazing scholar. He seemed to know everything there was to know about the medical industry. He'd met with many of the world's most distinguished scientists in person, sometimes arguing with these intellectual giants over nuances and minor imperfections in their published articles.

He was extremely perceptive.

Courtney felt a strange sensation she struggled to name. Maybe it was fear. For the first time since she was a rookie, she worried she might be exposed as a fraud. The doctor's intelligence was frightening.

Stealthily, she slipped a tiny, button-sized robot out of her pocket and dropped it to the floor. It scurried off, searching for a computer system to hack.

Finally, they reached his office. For the next hour, Courtney pretended to be a hardworking American journalist, peppering Watashi Shokan with eager questions about his career, contributions to science, and rapidly expanding business empire. Her cell phone recorded every sentence, and she scribbled furiously on a legal notepad.

However, she wasn't paying attention to his answers, not really. Her mind drifted. Silently, Courtney wondered whether this impressive and effusively charming surgeon was a criminal mastermind. Whether she was going to murder him. Part of her hoped he was guilty so she could finish this investigation soon. The other side of her was drawn to Dr. Shokan and wanted him to be innocent. He was a fascinating millionaire.

And he was very attractive.

She felt tremendous guilt for thinking he was handsome. It felt like emotional adultery, an unforgivable betrayal of the memory of her husband. Marcus deserved better than to be forgotten.

Courtney decided to take a risk to entrap the doctor.

"I've been considering paying for plastic surgery," she said. "Cosmetic surgery interests me because I've always wanted to improve my face, my body. What do you think, Dr. Shokan? What could a man like you do to help me?"

The surgeon frowned, and despite his perceptiveness, he didn't seem to grasp the suggestive nature of her questions.

"Nothing is perfect," he said at last. "But in your case, I strongly recommend avoiding surgery. That advice goes against my financial interests, but I'm already wealthy and you're gorgeous. You don't need to alter your appearance."

"I appreciate that," said Courtney. "Anyway, that was my last question for you. Thanks again for your time. You can expect my profile on your historic role in cosmetic surgery to be printed in a couple of months."

They both stood.

"Before you leave, I'd like to ask you a question," Dr. Shokan said. "Would you like to have dinner with me tonight?"

Watashi Shokan's computer system was hacked as soon as Courtney left the building. Medical companies rarely sought out the kind of private sector cybersecurity that could withstand the CIA's most effective military tech. Courtney reviewed the results with a team of analysts. They didn't find anything illegal. He was clean.

"You don't need to go on your date anymore," teased one of the analysts, and everyone started laughing. Except Courtney. Coldly, she glared at the low-ranking agents, until the room became awkwardly silent.

"Put surveillance on the other two suspects," Courtney said brusquely. "Let's get some results. We need to wrap up this investigation." Then she left.

Conflicting emotions filled her. Flirting with the handsome surgeon had been a smart tactical move when there was a possibility she needed to kill him. Bringing him to her hotel room would have provided an easy way to dispose of his body. But now that Courtney knew Watashi was innocent, the deadly agent no longer felt sure about what outcome she desired. Did she want to date him?

Tokyo was magnificent at night. The streets came alive in the evening, swarming with crowds of dark-haired pedestrians. All around her gleamed the neon magenta of billboards, the fast ivory-white flares of tourist cameras, the steady amber dullness of streetlamps, and the green-yellow-red of traffic lights performing their endless vigil. Courtney had been to New York, and the feeling of clutter and constant activity was similar, only Tokyo was more colorful. She weaved past storefronts and parked cars, inhaling the smog of cigarettes, barbeque, and ammonia cleaning fluid.

Tokyo had a profound effect on Courtney. Here was grandeur on a massive scale, both depressing and inspirational. Next to the splendor of Tokyo, Courtney seemed tiny. She felt swallowed up, lost in this alien ecosystem.

Tokyo symbolized the history, beauty, and elegance of Eastern tradition reinforced by Western technology. It was a magnificent palace of modern globalization. Walking the streets of this sleek, radiant metropolis felt like swimming through the bloodstream of a mechanized leviathan.

Unsure of her own motivations, Courtney met Watashi Shokan on the balcony of an extravagant restaurant beneath an indoor waterfall. The surgeon looked quite dashing in a tuxedo. And she was stunning as well, clothed in a long glittering gown of fiery crimson. Together, they feasted on battered spider rolls, roasted duck, skewers of shrimp and soft-shell crab meat, cucumbers, and a delicious broth of squid, ginger, and tuna. They talked for a while.

Later, in his bedroom, when he cried out "Danielle!" she almost hit him. But it wasn't his fault; that was her alias.

There were pictures of another woman in his bedroom. Over the course of an hour, Courtney knocked them off the walls, the dresser, and the cabinets like a tiger claiming her territory. She pretended it was an accident. Either she was a good actress or Watashi saw through her feigned clumsiness and just didn't care.

After a few hours of physical exertion, they began to talk again.

"Who's the woman in your pictures?" Courtney asked. It was a sloppy mistake. A good operative never revealed her true feelings to anyone. But she was jealous.

"My ex-wife," Watashi admitted. He wore a strange tired expression. He seemed beaten down by failure or regret. "Sometimes I think about her. We were happy for a while. Now she hates me and she's remarried. As an insult, I received an invitation to her wedding. But I don't hate her. Not anymore."

Watashi lifted his chin, calmly meeting Courtney's eyes. "There's a sadness to you, my flower of the West. Some kind of insecurity. I recognize it because I feel the same way. To be vulnerable is difficult. Our world has been built on masks."

"You're a surgeon," Courtney said angrily. She resented his perceptiveness. "Your knife cuts and sculpts meat like a common butcher. Leave the psychology to someone else. What would a person like you know about masks, anyway?"

Watashi shrugged. "Less than some, more than others . . . because I manufacture them. Every day I craft new masks. Identity is malleable. I'm an artist at the core, for all artists are liars, and my deceptions are lovely. Clients come to me searching for more than a different face, a tighter waist, or perky silicon breasts. What they actually crave is a new life. And I provide that illusion."

"Just my luck," Courtney said wryly. "Cute guy, amazing date, and then at the end of the night, he reveals he's built his career on being dishonest."

Watashi laughed. "Not exactly." He kissed her, and she lay in his arms, carefree. She felt safe. "Don't take that too literally. It's more of a metaphor. Think about how storytelling blurs facts and manipulates audience perception. Sometimes there are deeper truths we can't articulate. Plastic surgery is a symptom of modern insecurities. Nobody believes they are good enough anymore."

Courtney had never considered that before. But he was right. What kind of culture produces celebrities, entrepreneurs, and executives who are uniformly miserable? It was the same in America. The rich were victims of their own impossible standards. They gained no satisfaction, no pride, and no fulfillment from their finest achievements. Something was wrong. There were so many benefits that came from global improvements in education and prosperity and the exponential growth in living standards. But a bleak spiritual desolation gnawed at the roots. Shallow materialism warped the beauty and dignity of civilization into something gross, an endless hunger that could never be pleased. Consumerism was always chasing, always agitating, never content.

Courtney saw the same emptiness in herself. Everything that made her an effective spy also made her a terrible person. Coldness, paranoia, and a lack of remorse. Since her husband's funeral, she'd been depressed and self-destructive. The dangers of this assignment mostly helped her forget her sadness and pain, but violence was an unhealthy way to process grief.

Courtney knew what she feared. Working for the CIA kept her busy, gave her something to do. But being a good wife had been the core of her identity. Without some kind of purpose steering her, Courtney was afraid she'd fall apart. She didn't know a better alternative. Sinking back into the quicksand of alcohol wasn't an option.

That night, Courtney dreamed she was on a beach, watching the sunset. Strong arms held her, and she leaned back happily, bracing herself against the hard, reassuring firmness of a man's chest. A masculine voice whispered in her ears, the deep rumble of a baritone, and the man told her that he loved her. Courtney grinned. He belonged to her, and this was bliss; here was everything she'd ever desired.

In the morning, when Courtney awakened, she couldn't remember whether it had been Marcus or Watashi holding her in the dream.

Burning with shame, the agent dressed and left the surgeon's mansion.

For the next week, Courtney buried herself in work. Watashi tried to contact her, but she ignored his texts and phone calls. Reading surveillance reports was less confusing than trying to sift through her emotions and guess at what she actually wanted from him. Smuggling firearms into Tokyo and mapping out attack routes was more tangible and much simpler to understand.

But it ran deeper than that. Courtney wasn't ready to be honest with herself.

Her surveillance operation identified their enemy much faster than she'd expected. One of the clinics they were observing serviced an abnormally high frequency of foreigners. Most of these patients were French or American, but a small number were bearded Arabs or scowling, heavily scarred men from the Balkans. The practice was owned by Hidari Kagaku, a renowned surgeon in his late fifties.

After two weeks of spying on small fish, the CIA caught a whale.

An ordinary taxi pulled up to the clinic, nothing special. Out of it stepped one of the most famous faces in terrorism, an Iranian general named Qasem Soleimani, followed by a pair of alert muscular bodyguards. He was the Babe Ruth of body counts. The devil himself.

At a glance, Soleimani didn't look like a fearsome warrior. He was a short, thin old man who walked with a slight limp, a reminder of his wound from the Iran–Iraq war thirty years before. But this small, unimposing scarecrow with chronic back pain had controlled the destiny of the Middle East for the past decade.

Entrusted with Iran's foreign policy, Qasem Soleimani had been the mastermind behind hundreds of bombings and assassinations, everywhere from Brazil to Israel. It had been Qasem Soleimani and his battle-hardened soldiers who saved the Syrian dictator Assad from collapse. And there was no doubt that American blood stained his hands. Hundreds of American soldiers had been killed, and thousands more wounded beyond recognition, by the roadside bombs he supplied to Iraqi guerillas. He was the most brilliant military strategist in the Middle East, a source of mayhem and destruction.

And now he was here, vulnerable in Japan. There was a narrow window of opportunity to eliminate him.

Agents radioed that Qasem Soleimani had been spotted. He was buying a new face.

Courtney considered her options. For the rest of her career, there would never be another shot like this. There would never be an enemy of this importance and strategic value so close to her, so easy to kill. How she handled this chance would define her.

Courtney paced back and forth in the cheap apartment the CIA had rented for her subordinates. One order from Courtney could send thirty trained killers into that clinic. She would be a hero, and one of America's worst enemies—a legendary commander who had dominated an entire continent with secret wars and genocide—would be dead.

But there would be a tremendous cost to a direct attack. A couple of her men would die in the ensuing firefight, as well as probably a few dozen Japanese citizens. The alliance between America and Japan would be permanently damaged due to the scandal of an illegal CIA kill team running amok, murdering innocent civilians in the crossfire of an unauthorized raid. And more American soldiers would die in Iraq from landmines supplied by the Iranian military. Qasem Soleimani was a national hero in Iran, a symbol of courage and power, and Iran would inevitably retaliate to save face.

"Stand down," said Courtney. "Rent a few taxis so we can tail Soleimani when he leaves. Find out where he's staying. While he's in surgery, we'll have a couple of hours to prepare a proper welcome. And above all, don't lose him. If I see anyone blunder on this, you can kiss your pension goodbye."

Courtney waited until midnight to move on the surgeon Hidari Kagaku. He was at the home of his mistress. That made him easier to blackmail.

Three burly agents followed Courtney inside, carrying heavy satchels of equipment. They were dressed as a team of electricians. The trick to any good burglary was to look like you belonged.

Courtney found the surgeon and his mistress on a sofa, mostly undressed. "What are you doing inside my house?" shouted Hidari Kagaku. He struggled to climb to his feet, but two of the agents leaped forward and pinned him to the couch. They began beating him professionally, savagely punching his ribs and clinically smashing everything except his head and the precious hands that his trade depended on. The other agent pulled the mistress away.

"I have a better question," Courtney said sharply. "Why would you disguise a criminal like Qasem Soleimani?"

Kagaku's face whitened.

"You have two options," Courtney explained in a reasonable tone. "You can become an informant. That means you will turn over your files on every terrorist you've operated on so my government can hunt them down. Your business will continue to function, but only as a trap. If you refuse, we'll murder you and stage your death as a suicide."

Courtney pulled out a pistol and gestured with her other hand. The weeping mistress was thrown to the floor. Without blinking, Courtney raised her arm and fired a bullet into the woman's skull.

"Feel free to go to the police," said Courtney. "Your fingerprints cover this crime scene. I can see the headlines tomorrow: Wealthy Doctor Murders Lover."

Hidari Kagaku sobbed but said nothing.

"Make him clean this mess," said Courtney. "That will help him remember the price of mistakes." Disgusted, she turned away and walked outside.

Early in the morning, an Iranian general was killed by a car bomb. Nobody in Tokyo could figure out why the Iranian commander had traveled to Japan or who had assassinated him. Bombs didn't leave much evidence.

There was a buzzing in Courtney's pocket. She looked at her phone. Watashi Shokan was calling her. She answered.

A few days later, they met on a train to Hiroshima.

"I've missed you, Danielle," admitted Watashi. "You've captivated me ever since the first interview."

Sliding into his arms, Courtney decided to be as honest as she could. "My real name is Courtney."

They talked for hours. Watashi adored her bright smile, how her lips pouted seriously when she was making a point, and the endearing roughness of her Japanese. She didn't have an accent, but there were a lot of aphorisms and allusions she couldn't understand because they referenced stories in Japanese literature she hadn't read or historical events she didn't know. Courtney was relieved the doctor wasn't angry with her for ignoring him or for lying about her name. He was so happy to see her again.

Watashi took her on a tour of Hiroshima. It was a gorgeous city with a fair climate. Euphorically, she basked in the landscape of museums, shrines, parks, stadiums, and theaters. Together, they admired the crisp architecture of Carp Castle, a replica fortress that had been reconstructed after the surrender of Japan.

Eventually, the tour led to where Courtney knew it must, a memorial to everyone killed by the atomic bomb. As they strolled through the well-trimmed gardens beside Genbaku Dome, it was impossible for Courtney not to reflect on the heavy cost of war and the damage she'd inflicted on the CIA's enemies over the years. It was an emotional place. Courtney wondered if her life had made the world a better place.

Probably not.

"I brought you here because I care about you," said Watashi. "This is not the most romantic site to take a date, but it's very meaningful."

Courtney stared at him. "My husband died a few months ago. I think maybe I tried to be a different person. Sometimes numbness is easier than feeling pain. But I need help. I don't like myself anymore."

"I'm here for you," promised Watashi, and he hugged her tightly. That was all he needed to say.

Deep in thought, Courtney assessed the city around her. She had lost her best friend this year. Marcus was gone. But compared to the fallout of an atomic bomb, the death of a spouse seemed almost unimportant. Somehow, Hiroshima was prosperous and thriving.

And that was the lesson of Hiroshima. People have enough resilience to recover from any tragedy. Grief doesn't need to last forever. Cities can be rebuilt, and broken hearts can heal. There was so much Courtney could choose to live for. Marcus had shared the best years of her life, and she'd lost him. But maybe she could learn to love again.

Courtney looked at Watashi Shokan. For the first time in a long time, she was happy imagining her future.

Franklin called her that night to congratulate her. The Iranian general was dead, the Japanese surgeon was compromised, and the CIA was pleased. Franklin mentioned there was an assignment in Italy that would be perfect for her.

Respectfully, Courtney declined. She planned to stay in Japan for a while.

Rhyme and Reason

Dorothy Tinker

"Vivid Forest shines its forbidding light,
Against Plains we made our home.
Crimson River burns and no more bears life,
While Desert kills all who roam."

I stare at my parents from my place at their feet. They sit side-by-side on the shadowed hearth of our stone and grass home. Their heads are bent together, their foreheads just touching. Their hair, nearly the same shade as the skin it frames, mingles until I can't tell whose is whose. Their lips stir against each other as they repeat the nightly litany like a beloved nursery rhyme.

A *twisted* nursery rhyme.

Then, as one of them does every night, my mother turns to me and lays a hand on my shoulder. "Remember these words, child. They are our life."

Our life?

"Why?"

Suddenly, there is no longer a hand on my shoulder. My mother's eyes are wide as she shakes her head and leans back against my father's shoulder. When she speaks, her voice is faint.

"Ours is not to question the words of our ancestors, child."

"Why not?"

My mother turns and buries her head against my father's neck, and my father wraps his arms around her. Neither answer me. My father doesn't even look at me. His eyes stare above me, but it is only when he bows his head that I turn to see what he was looking at.

We no longer sit in our own home but instead stand in the village center, surrounded by numerous small buildings made of stone and grass. However, it's the elder behind me, looming over my small form, who holds my attention. His clothes are made from the same brown hide as the rest of the villagers', but his face marks him out, with wrinkled skin and long gray hair. His pale brown eyes, so similar to mine, my parents', and everyone else's, are sharp as stone knives as he glares down at me.

"Mind your words, child!"

His grating voice is harsh against my ears, burning through them the way the Crimson River burns through life. But frustration fills my chest and swells up my throat. "Why?" I snap. "Why aren't we allowed to question? Why does the Forest shine? Why—"

Crack!

Pain blooms across my cheek and burns through my neck. Black spots threaten my vision, followed by salty wetness that touches my lips almost as quickly as it does my eyes. The taste of metal, however, overwhelms the salt.

When I can see again, I turn back to the elder. His pale eyes glare narrowly at my parents, not me.

"Teach your child the evils of such curiosity, or we will bestow the ultimate punishment."

My parents bow and scrape and apologize until the elder turns away and leaves the village center. Only then does my mother turn back to me, her own eyes narrowed and lined as they meet my wide gaze. There is anger there, but the slump of her shoulders and the quiver of her chin betray her disappointment.

Disappointment that drives through me and urges me to apologize—not for questioning, but for making her feel such emotions.

"Mother—"

Smack!

Pain bursts across my other cheek, a perfect match for the first.

"The ultimate punishment, child! Do you even understand what that means?"

I clench my teeth. My cheeks ache, liquid copper fills my mouth, and tears slide down my cheeks, but I refuse to show her the pain that swells within my chest. Burying it deep beneath anger and curiosity, I shake my head.

"Banishment!" She glances around as though in search of listening ears. I don't follow her gaze. I know there is no one else around. "The ultimate punishment is banishment to the Forest!"

My whole body unclenches. "Really? You mean I could go into the Forest? I want—"

She gives a quiet scream and throws her hands into the air, raising her eyes to the heavens. "It's forbidden, child! Why can't you accept that? Why must you continue to question the words of our ancestors?"

I jut out my chin and cross my arms. "Because I want to know. I don't understand how you can just accept the words so blindly."

She straightens up and frowns down at me. "I accept them because they are our life, child." Grabbing my arm, she drags me back toward our home. "And I suggest you do the same."

"No!" I tug against her grip. "I want to know! I want to go into the Forest! I want—"

She releases my arm so abruptly, I drop to the ground. Looming over me, she hisses, "If you keep this up, you will be banished. You will be banished and never allowed to return. The only reason the elder spares you now is that you are too young to know better." Shaking her head, she turns away. I hear her speak one final time before she walks away, her words so despairing that the pain returns to my chest, unbidden.

"You won't always be too young."

I wake with an ache in my chest and tears in my eyes. Growling, I scrub at my eyes with my fists and ignore the familiar pain. It is not the first time the dream has come to me, as old memories refuse to leave me be.

Memories that have only grown more persistent in recent weeks.

Dropping my hands, I throw back my covers and swing my legs over the side of the bed. I take a deep breath of the crisp morning air and glance around my room. Beside my bed sits a small table; the wall holding the door across from me is taken up almost entirely by a squat set of drawers. Every piece of furniture is a patchwork of rough-hewn stone, tough grasses, and fired mud. The arrangement is old, but the stone pieces are nearly impossible to move without help.

Nobody is ever willing to help.

I turn my head to stare out the window at the foot of my bed. The sun has barely risen, and pinks and oranges still tint the eastern sky, where the flat Plains disappear straight out to the horizon. I wrinkle my nose. As always, I wish my window looked out to the south, where the Vivid Forest stands in the distance, its green vivacity taunting me with my lack of knowledge.

Maybe if my people dared to breach the Forest, we could make furniture from wood instead of stone. Then I wouldn't have to ask, and they wouldn't have to look at me with such...disdain...

The ache in my chest throbs again, and I struggle to bury it in the usual anger and curiosity. When it takes longer than a moment to call up enough of either, I shake my head vigorously.

"Stop it!" I snap quietly. "They're the ones who refuse to question. They're the ones who are content to live in the dull Plains while the Forest taunts us with its offerings of shade, wood, and who knows how many other—"

A gentle knock on my bedroom door interrupts my rant. Tamping down a snarl, I call for the knocker to enter. When the door opens, my mother cranes her head around its edge. Her eyes, so fiery in my dream, stare at me with dull exhaustion that weighs on my chest like the stone of my furniture.

"You're awake," she whispers, bobbing her head slightly. "Why don't you come have breakfast?"

She closes the door before I can answer, and I shiver. My mother was once so spirited. When I was younger and first began to question the law, she would yell at me and trade arguments with me more than anyone else could. But now . . .

"You won't always be too young."

I turn my head away from the door. My eyes land on the timepiece that stands upon my bedside table, one of the few technologies to survive from the time of our ancestors. It's a complex piece that not only displays the time of the day but also the time of the year. And it currently shows what I have been trying to avoid since I awoke.

Today is my birthday. My sixteenth birthday.

Today, I am old enough for the ultimate punishment.

Breakfast is a hodgepodge of my favorite foods: small pond fish coated in my mother's best sauce, wild beets tossed with honeysuckle nectar, and a chunk of honeycomb nearly the size of my fist. The presumptive allusion that this might very well be my last meal sparks a fire in my throat that prevents me from doing anything but stare at the food on my plate.

"Aren't you going to eat, child?" my mother murmurs fretfully from my right.

I shake my head, keeping my eyes on my plate, but I can still see her expression in my mind. Deep lines encircle her eyes and lips, her brown eyes dark and dull. The corners of her lips droop down without effort, and her hands move incessantly, burying themselves in the folds of her shirt or tearing at the grass mat beneath her plate.

If I turn to her and see the weariness within her now, I don't know what will come out of my mouth.

"Eat," my father orders gruffly from my left. "Your mother worked hard to send you off properly."

I dare a glance in my father's direction, but his eyes are on the stone and chisel in his hands. He's a stoneworker for the village, and he's always busy with one task or another. That he hasn't looked at me since the first time an elder slapped me seems . . . natural.

Ignoring the twinge in my heart, I push the plate away. "I'm not hungry." The words are almost true. My stomach roils with anticipation, and I don't know if I'm looking forward to what's to come . . . or dreading it.

My mother's breath catches, but the sound is soft enough for me to ignore as I stand and return to my room. There's already a half-packed bag sitting on the squat set of drawers. I grab it and start shoving into it the few pieces of clothing I'm allowed to take with me: an extra shirt, an extra pair of pants, and a couple pieces of underwear.

I hesitate when I reach the socks that have made their way into one drawer. Living in the Plains, I've always worn light, open sandals. It was only a few days ago that my father came home with a pair of shoes that would fully cover my feet. He shoved them into my arms before plying himself to the work he'd brought home.

Later that night, I found my mother placing three pairs of socks in my drawers. When she caught me staring, she flushed. "Just in case."

Wetness strikes the back of my hand, bringing me back to the present. "Stop it!" I scrub my hands over my wet cheeks. Then I grab two pairs of socks and shove them into the bag. Before I can falter again, I grab the third pair from the drawer and turn to hunt down the new pair of shoes.

I find them sprawled against one corner of the room. After a few minutes of struggle, I manage to cram my feet into both the socks and the shoes. They feel strange and restrictive. I try to ignore the sensation, but it sets my whole body on edge.

Have I done the right thing?

I quickly hiss and chase the thought away. With the Forest and the answers I crave so close, now is not the time to question myself.

Despite my hurried packing, another two hours pass before a loud *thump* announces the arrival of the five elders and their cadre of warriors. Each man carries a spear pieced together from cane rods and animal bones. Each glares at me as I step from my home into their midst.

As they lead me away, a gasping sob reaches my ears, and I glance over my shoulder. My parents stand in the doorway of our home, their heads leaning so close together that their foreheads nearly touch. Tears slide down their cheeks, and they strain forward against the doorframe as though an invisible barrier keeps them from passing it.

In that moment, my father's eyes meet mine for the first time in years. They are darker than my mother's, but not as dull, and they don't hold the anger I've always expected. Instead, they appear cloudy, though with tears or something else, I don't know. Whatever it is, that haze pierces me, filling my stomach with rocks the way my mother's gaze fills my chest with stone.

Squeezing my eyes shut, I turn back around, only to falter in my stride as my mother yells a word I have not heard since I first began to question.

My name.

My throat tightens. I duck my head to hide the tears dancing in my eyes. I swallow, but the pain is too much. I cannot see my feet or the ground beneath them.

As I stagger, a heavy hand lands on my shoulder and directs my movements. "Perhaps you are beginning to understand the damage your questions have wrought, child."

I don't respond, and I doubt the elder expects me to. He knows I won't stop questioning the law, and I know my mother was right all those years ago.

The silence grows as we walk south toward the Forest, breathing and pacing alongside us like a living beast. Eventually, my eyes dry and my steps steady, but the silence doesn't abate. It only becomes grimmer as the elders and warriors lead me closer to a place so forbidden to our people.

The sun has climbed high above our heads by the time we stop.

Far to our right, out to the west, lies the Crimson River. At this distance, its waters shimmer beneath the high sun, appearing almost blue, and its ragged banks look almost smooth and natural.

On the other side of the River sprawls the killing Desert. If such an attribute fits it, I doubt anyone could prove it. The Crimson River burns all things—grass, stone, human flesh—so no one can reach the Desert to learn its nature. Why our ancestors even mentioned it in my people's beloved law is just another question to have stirred my curiosity all these years.

With River and Desert to my right, I face the south and the Vivid Forest that stands there, looming high above me and extending beyond sight to the east. To the west, it abuts the River but doesn't dare cross it. Briefly, I wonder if it, too, would question the Desert's nature.

Shaking my head, I drop the question and force myself to simply take in the sight before me. We've ventured so close now that I can make out individual leaves on many of the trees. I marvel at their beauty. I've never been this far south before. A sudden energy fills me, overwhelming the pain in my chest and stomach just enough for me to forget it.

As I examine the plants—towering trees with green-leafed branches and green-covered trunks and, at their base, curly, furling, soft-looking shrubs that I can hardly make out for their strangeness—one elder begins to recite the beloved law of our people. I ignore him. *Who cares about ancient laws when there's such beauty to be seen?*

The return of a hand upon my shoulder interrupts my basking, and I turn my head to glare at the elder. He glares right back.

"You have been accused of questioning the words of our ancestors, child. What do you say in response?"

I roll my eyes. "Why bother asking, elder? You know the answer better than anyone." *Even if it had changed, you wouldn't take me back.*

My breath threatens to catch in my throat, but I breathe carefully.

The elder sighs. I glance at him from the corner of my eye. For a single moment, he appears to slump. It must be a trick of my mind, though. When I turn to look at him fully, he stands tall and stern.

"As Head Elder of the Clan of Man, I banish you, child, into the Vivid Forest."

The hand on my shoulder shoves. I stumble forward several steps before regaining my balance. Not bothering to look back, I continue walking toward the Forest's edge.

From behind me, the elder's voice follows me into the Forest.

"May you find what you seek before the Forest destroys you."

The passage from open air to pressing green startles me. I hunch my shoulders and duck my head, dipping under hanging tree limbs and brushing past reaching undergrowth. It isn't long before I'm breathing thanks to my absent father for the new shoes. Bare, my feet would have been cut to ribbons within minutes of entering the Forest.

As I walk, I turn my head in all directions. Everything is so green! Despite the description of the Forest in our ancestors' words, I never expected the interior to be so . . . light! An unchanging paleness illuminates everything, and I marvel that the sun can reach through the dense trees so evenly.

The wonder, however, fades over time. Everything is green, and that green is *everywhere*. Even after hours of walking, even after I am sure the sun must have set, the green never changes, and neither does the pale illumination. The light and the green drive me on, even as tiredness drags at my eyes and exhaustion at my feet. I try to block them out by dropping my head and focusing only on my feet.

But that only enhances another difference between the Forest and the Plains I never expected.

Silence.

Once, I would have said true silence could be found at night in the middle of the Plains when no one roams and all creatures have settled to sleep. Yet that silence is full of the chirps of night insects, the whistle of wind through the tall grass, and the quiet laughter of the stars and moon.

This silence—the silence of the Forest—is filled with *nothing*. It weighs down on me and swallows every little sound, including my own breath. I would have thought the greenery itself would make noise, as the grass of the Plains does, but there is nothing but pressure in my ears and a distinct sense of . . . lack.

I picture the beast of silence I imagined following us from the village to the Forest, its body like a large cat, its tail whipping back and forth. It seems a measly thing now compared to the monster of silence surrounding me here. Its breath is like ice upon my neck, the touch of its gaze like fire. I have no reference for such ideas, but I picture sweeping wings arching to the canopy, muffling everything, and a drifting tail that touches upon the surrounding greenery but refuses to disturb it.

I shiver and begin to whistle, hoping to drive back the beast in my mind, but like my breath, the high-pitched sound quickly disappears among the trees. Licking my lips, I cast my gaze to either side, but there remains nothing but greenery and that incessant pale light.

Just as I return my attention to my feet—and where they might land beneath the thick underbrush—a piercing noise breaks the silence. Gasping, I clap my hands to my ears and stumble forward, my heart suddenly racing. I want to run, but even as I try to quicken my pace, the toe of one of my restrictive shoes catches on something unseen and I sprawl into the bushes.

The sharp sound repeats, and I cry out against the pain in my ears. Unlike the new sound, my cry is still muffled by the oppressive winged monster of silence.

When it comes again—a high-pitched burst, like a mockery of my earlier attempts to whistle—I clamber to my feet and run as fast as I can through catching branches and entangling leaves. I stumble time and again as my feet hit invisible obstacles, but the high-pitched sounds fill my ears and my mind, and I can think of nothing but the need to escape them.

My breathing grows ragged. My face, arms, and legs hurt from the snapping branches that impede my path. My feet throb, but still I pound on, too terrified of what lies behind me to listen to my body's demands for rest.

Then the world tilts.

I stumble again. This time, instead of scrambling to my feet and continuing on, I can do nothing but fall.

And I continue to fall.

I crash through branches and leaves, tumbling wildly, and I can't tell if I'm falling through trees, air, or underbrush. I twist and turn, trying to catch myself upon something, if only to slow my progress, but I can't differentiate up from down nor left from right, and everything slips through my fingers. My awareness narrows to this single motion, until all I know is falling.

Until all I know is green and pain.

I don't know when the world stills, or even how long I lie in that stillness. Only slowly do I become aware…

Aware of a steady pressure against my chest and stomach . . .

Aware of an uncomfortable twist in my legs . . .

Aware of a steady, pulsing pressure in my ears . . .

It takes me even longer to become aware of my surroundings. All I see is the unchanging green and incessant pale light that has encompassed me since I first entered the Forest. I close my eyes to block it out, but the place behind my eyes is no longer the darkness I am accustomed to. It glows with a dim, pale light, revealing green even there.

A sob wrenches from my throat, muffled by the silence, and I peel my eyes open. I don't want to be here. I don't want to be in this forest of green, with its unchanging light and living silence. I want to go home, to burrow into my mother's embrace, to beg my father to look at me until all I see is the darkness of his eyes and the brown of his cheeks. I want to beg their forgiveness.

"I'll accept the ways of our people," I mutter against the crook of my elbow. The words barely reach my ears. "I'll accept the words of our ancestors."

Anything to keep the green and light and silence from invading my mind and overtaking my self.

"May you find what you seek before the Forest destroys you."

I sob again. The Forest is already destroying me, and I don't even know what I seek or where I can find it. All I want is to go back, but I don't know which way is north or if the Forest would even release me now that is has me.

Abruptly, the pressure in my ears increases until I can make out sounds. I snap my head up and listen, ignoring the pain that radiates down my back from my neck. I strain to hear, and I quickly realize that the deep, pulsing sound is a drumbeat.

My heart stutters within my chest, and ice prickles down my back. There's someone else in this forest!

As I listen, the drums grow louder and wilder, and my heart picks up the beat. For the first time in years, the pain and anger rooted in my chest drift away, and only pure curiosity stirs within me.

Who is it? Who could possibly make the Forest their home? Do they know why the Forest is forbidden? Could they possibly know why the River burns and the Desert is referenced in the law?

As these questions fill my mind, I pull myself up onto my hands and knees and stumble to my feet. Pain strikes up my legs, but my curiosity is far too great for me to ignore. I limp forward, certain the drumbeat is calling from this direction. It pounds through me, drives me, and I know it will not steer me wrong.

As I stagger toward the sound, the trees and the underbrush seem to part before me. They welcome me like old friends, directing me toward my new home and bidding me stay. I grin and hurry my step.

The drumbeat is soon joined by other sounds, and they flow around me like a soothing river. They lap at my mind calmingly, though when I try to really *hear* them, all I can understand is simple serenity.

By the time I see colors other than the unchanging green, I'm fully content, and I only smile. Red flits here. Blue appears there. Purple rises up from the ground to my right, while a bright burst of orange and yellow settles on my left, so reminiscent of the sun that I turn my face and half-close my eyes to bask in its light and heat.

"You should have stayed in the Plains, Manling."

I blink as the words filter through my ears. I'm suddenly aware that I've stopped moving, and the colors surrounding me seem to have multiplied. A flutter begins in my chest, but the contentment rises up and swallows it.

"I was banished," I whisper, certain that is the answer to the words my mind is still interpreting.

"Banished?" The voice speaks the word slowly as though tasting it. "Why would Man send one of their own into a place where they do not belong?"

I blink again and frown. Something's not right. Whoever addresses me speaks of men as if he were not one himself.

"I . . . wanted to come." My frown deepens, and I close my eyes. Those aren't the right words.

"Why?"

I open my eyes and stare. The voice is coming from straight ahead, but all I see is green, purple, and a darkness beyond black. I try to force the image to make sense, but the shapes don't match what should be there.

"Why?" the voice repeats, insistent.

I shake my head. *Perhaps understanding will come later. Like with the law.*

"Exactly."

Silence follows my response, so deep that I imagine the winged, tailed monster pacing behind me.

"Exactly . . . ?" The voice sounds uncertain, so very different from its earlier strength.

I nod. "Exactly. 'Why' is exactly my reason for coming to the Forest. I questioned the law."

The darkness beyond black moves closer, and breath like fire stirs upon my face. "Law? Tell me, Manling. What questions did you ask?"

I stare, unblinking, into that darkness. I vaguely remember a wish to look upon the darkness of my absent father's eyes, but this darkness seems better. I can lose myself within this darkness in a way I couldn't with my father's eyes.

"Why is the Forest forbidden?" I whisper. "Why does the River burn? Why did the ancestors speak of the Desert when no one can reach it? Why—"

I grunt as an oppressive pain burns up my throat. I try to ignore it, to speak what my curiosity demands to know, but something has stilled the breath in my lungs. My lips gape wide, but my throat refuses to stir.

"Man is insolent!" the voice hisses. I try to apologize, but again my breath won't come. "You take the words of our lament and twist them to your own purpose. You, who made the world the way it is, would act as victims?"

I shake my head weakly. There's black at the edge of my vision, black that makes the darkness before me even darker. *I don't,* I mouth, but I don't think the darkness understands.

"Do you want answers, Manling? Do you want to know *why* the world is the way it is?"

I want to nod, but the pain in my throat is growing unbearable and I don't think I can move.

"Listen to our lament, Manling. Listen and learn."

And as the world narrows to the darkness before me and the black around my vision, the soothing river of sounds rises around me until I can finally hear its words—its lament:

"To light Forest, he banished us from home,
Through empty Plains ruled by Man.
He destroyed the Desert, from whence we roam,
And with blood, the River ran."

The familiarity of the words strikes through me more strongly than the pain and stillness in my lungs. I struggle to fit them to the words I know, the words that have been my life, but they refuse. My body sways from my neck down and my gut churns.

My people live a lie. They live a lie, and they will do anything to protect that lie.

The despair sinks deep within me, digging its claws within my heart and tearing through my brain. It sinks so deeply within me that I can find no relief from it.

And yet I seek relief.

"Why?" I whisper, somehow finding breath to propel the word past chapped lips. "Why did—"

No relief. Not even in the screaming shock of pain that shoots down my spine . . . or in the enclosing wings of the monster of silence . . . or in the darkness that follows it all.

Ticket for One

Lee Ann Rozek

*W*hat is that? I haven't heard it before—this . . . pulsing or maybe chugging and whirring? The last thing I remember was drifting off to sleep with my family by my bedside. I haven't heard this particular noise since being admitted to the hospital; perhaps I'm imagining things?

Nope! There's that sound again! It's not loud, per se, but also not faint or difficult to hear once focused on. I wonder what generates such a rhythmic sound? Oh, I remember now; it reminds me of that train trip I took through the Smoky Mountains! The cool, crisp air and mountain views took my breath away! I remember thinking how enormous the mountains appeared while the train steamed through gorgeous woodlands showcasing the vibrant brilliance of fall.

I certainly don't remember boarding a train, though. What an odd situation; I have no recollection of buying a ticket or mounting stairs to reach the platform, yet I can hear what sounds like a train and muffled bits of conversation. There's even a slight swaying motion, now that I think about it.

I almost feel like I am back on that train, though! That train ride through the Smoky Mountains was a first for me. Growing up in the flat marshy area of the Texas Coastal Plain meant that if it wasn't grass, mud, water, or a scrubby tree, it was a novelty. Years ago, when I booked my trip, I was unsure whether my idea of travel qualified as true travel. When I heard people talk about traveling, it conjured up visions of rare continents and exotic animals—not the backwoods of Tennessee. That was my first trip out of Texas, ever. I had always dreamed of traveling, but the mortgage, the bills, and the kids' needs took priority.

I was in my fifties when I traveled to Tennessee. Anxiety battled with childlike excitement as I set out on my journey, but the airport provided endless entertainment. All those strangers, some running while others meandered, reminded me of an anthill. Granted, the idea of speeding through the air in a flying biscuit can jam-packed with over one hundred strangers was not appealing, but once I was on the plane and in the air, I started to relax and daydream about the adventure I'd started.

When I stepped out of the baggage claim area into the refreshing fall air, I thought I'd died and gone to heaven! In Texas, the heat beat us about the head and neck well into November some years, so finding temperatures in the sixties with low humidity during early October was a rare treat!

I had planned my trip so I could see what people meant when they talked about fall colors. In the coastal plains of Texas, all we had were pine trees that have two colors for their needles: green and brown, neither of which evoke words of wonder regarding their poetic beauty. On the ride to the hotel, the amount and variation of red, yellow, and orange leaves captivated me! Leaves—actual leaves—and they were more than green or brown! I imagine some might consider the fall color change in tree leaves less than spectacular, but for me this was a storybook come to life!

There was another sight I had only seen in textbooks or read about in novels: rock. No, not the pea gravel trucked in for landscaping purposes. I mean the sort of rock that nothing grows on and requires blasting to make roadways! Entire freeways bisected fifteen-foot (and taller) rock formations that contained their own beautiful colors in multiple layers. While others might recall the sapphire waters of Greece with fond reverence, nature's gifts of weather, rocks, and leaves changed the paradigm of the world's beauty in my eyes.

I no longer hear the muffled conversations from before. The rhythmic sound is still present but much slower than before. Come to think of it, the soft swaying motion of the train has gone away too. Perhaps I've found myself in the middle of a lucid dream. Yes! That would explain why I don't remember buying a ticket or boarding a train yet found myself feeling as though I was riding that same train from my trip to Tennessee all those years ago.

If I am dreaming, that could explain why I feel like I'm squished and confined in a dark space, since dreams make little sense upon waking. Come to think of it, I cannot see anything, not even the hand in front of my face. I am dreaming; that is the only explanation for my current situation. I'm sure when I wake up, I will be right where I fell asleep, in a hospital bed surrounded by my family. However, this dark, cramped feeling reminds me of my trip to New York, when the subway got stuck in a tunnel.

I traveled to New York a few years after my visit to Tennessee, and as someone who grew up in Texas, an underground train was an experience I had to try. Granted, the folks that use the subway daily probably think nothing of getting on a train with hundreds of strangers, but to me it was a once-in-a-lifetime experience. I couldn't wait to try it!

Traveling is often viewed and judged based on destination, but I think traveling should take the journey into consideration as well. I remember arriving in New York via airplane, then taking a cab to my hotel. The traffic, noise, and sheer volume of people was eye opening. A veritable cornucopia of humanity stretched out as far as the eye could see while my cab swerved, surged, and sputtered through the city.

After checking into my room, I was ready to venture out into the city. I found the closest subway station, bought my ticket, and eagerly waited for my train. I planned to ride toward Times Square, to take in that oft-talked-about area. I had only seen New York City via television broadcasts and didn't understand the less-mentioned realities of the city, like rats, blaring horns, bike messengers who were more kamikaze than messenger, and the gruff nature of native New Yorkers. While I was a little surprised by all of this, traveling has always been an adventure and the best adventures have surprises, sensory-overloading experiences, and sometimes gritty reality.

The train I needed clanked and wheezed into the boarding area, and I entered a car. I guess it was a popular route, as people kept packing into the car until we were all standing or sitting close enough to know what everyone else had eaten for breakfast. The train whined and rattled into motion and was soon rocketing us through dark tunnels sprinkled with lights, which plunged the car into darkness punctuated with brief flashes of light. The train slowed, and I thought, *Good, the ride is almost over!*

Wrong. The train ground to a halt in a pitch-black stretch of tunnel. I couldn't see my hand when touching my own nose, the dark was so complete. Some passengers yelled, others cussed; the rest let out a world-weary sigh but otherwise sat quietly. While getting stuck on the subway was not on my list of things to do in New York, this made telling people about my trip more interesting.

After what felt like an eternity but was probably closer to ten minutes, the power graced us with its return, allowing the train to arthritically resume its route. Upon reaching my destination, I dashed up the stairs to reach street level. The sun's glare was so brilliant, I could not see at first. It took my eyes a few seconds to adjust.

I stared agog at the scene before me. Times Square was packed to the edge of explosion with enormous screens advertising everything from clothing to investment options, while the crawlers disgorged a never-ending litany of the latest news and events. Of course, I stood still a little too long and was reminded by a passerby that I was not in Texas anymore when they bumped into me and then crassly explained that I should move. Ah, local authenticity, all part and parcel of the adventure, I guess.

I made my way through Times Square, taking photos as I went. The crush of people, noise, and aromas was overwhelming! These activities and sights might have seemed pedestrian to some, but I loved every minute of it! Like all the adventures I embarked upon, New York broadened my view of the world outside of Texas, and I felt richer for it.

That New York trip was one of my all-time favorite adventures. Remembering it puts a smile on my face, but I still can't figure out why I am in the dark feeling like a sardine in an upside-down can. I can hear muffled voices and that rhythmic noise again, but now the pulsing noise is faster and the voices sound urgent. This is the damnedest dream I have ever had; what are they giving me in this hospital to cause such a lucid dream?

For the life of me, I can hardly move; I feel like I'm upside down and the walls are closing in slowly. I'm starting to panic! My head and shoulders are being squeezed with such force that I know I will be crushed to death any minute! Oh my God, I'm going to die! This pressure is like nothing I can remember ever happening to me. How am I going to survive?

The voices are getting louder, the pulsing noise has assumed a jackhammer rhythm, and it feels like I'm being forced through a cylinder that is three sizes too small.

Wait! I can sort of see! Yes, the blackness is fading, but the bone-sliding pressure keeps intensifying; now my arms are pinned to my sides, and I can't move my legs as they've been stretched out completely straight. I can hear a woman screaming. Or am I screaming? I don't know how much more I can take before I will be crushed to death.

Now something is touching my head! What the hell is touching my head? Why can I hear excited voices beneath a calm command to push? Those are fingers around my head! What sort of nightmare am I in?

My entire head is now cold, my vision is overwhelmed by the light, and the cacophony of noise is terrifying! There is a hand wrapped around my neck, pulling my shoulders free, and now my entire body is freezing. All I can see is bright light, and all I can hear is people cheering, crying, voicing their congratulations.

I can feel one hand supporting my bottom and one hand

supporting my head while I scream for help. The hands are only tight enough to hold me, but how big must they be to support a five-foot-seven, 160-pound woman?

At least the crushing pressure I thought would kill me has stopped, though.

Now, I'm being rubbed roughly with some cloth, and I can hear a man asking, "Is she ok? How much does she weigh?" The light still blinds me, and I continue to scream for help, hoping someone will save me. The light dims, my eyes adjust, and I blurrily see a person standing on either side of me. Both are smiling, and the man keeps saying, "Hi, honey, it's okay; I'm right here."

The woman has a determined look on her face as she rubs me with that cloth and then puts some contraption in her ears while holding a cold metal thing against my chest.

Now I'm being wrapped in a blanket. The woman puts what feels like a stocking hat on my head and picks me up as though I weigh nothing. I'm passed off to the man, who holds me in his arms close enough that I can sort of see his face. He's smiling, and it looks like he might be crying too, but he says, "Hey, little girl, are you ready to meet your mom?"

I scream again. "*What?* Mom? I turned seventy-six this year. I'm not a little girl and haven't been one in a long time, and my mother died years ago! I have grown children of my own, and grandchildren!"

Never mind that I have absolutely no idea who this man is; he is certainly not my father!

This dream must end soon. How long can it go on, and so vividly? The man has now placed me in the arms of a new woman, who is smiling and crying. Her hair is sweaty and messy, but she keeps repeating, "Oh my, she is so perfect. I love you!"

I start screaming again, but the woman holding me calmly says, "It's okay, honey. Mommy has you." She rocks me gently and makes other soothing sounds. This woman is not my mother; she looks nothing like my mother, or even me for that matter.

My vision remains blurry, but I can see that I am swaddled in a blanket, just like my children were when I gave birth to them. How big are these people that they can hold someone my size in their arms? How do I end this dream? How do I wake myself up? Maybe if I can remember what was happening before I fell asleep, my logical brain will engage and I'll wake up in my hospital room.

I remember being in the hospital before I fell asleep and this crazy dream started. My children and grandchildren were there. We laughed and joked like usual, but I wasn't feeling well. The doctors had suggested I make final plans with my family related to my declining organ function and some hard-to-say word that described my blood tests, but I had paid little attention to them, considering I'd lived through worse.

The grandkids were tired, so I told my kids to go home for the night and that I would see them in the morning. That's right! The nurse came in and said "Good night" about nine o'clock last night. I must have drifted off to sleep and this dream began.

Except I should have been awakened by now by something, even if only my own bladder—never mind the nurse or the nurse's assistant (damned people come into my hospital room every hour). Yet I'm still wrapped up in a pink and blue blanket, being held by a woman calling me Evelyn.

Evelyn is my first name, but for some reason everyone has always called me by my middle name, Scarlett.

The man from earlier is standing over us, talking to someone and telling them to come to St. Luke's downtown and ask for room 408. Wait! I'm in St. Luke's downtown, but my room number is 1204. Obviously, I'm still dreaming; why else would I be wrapped up like a newborn baby?

Am I having a dream within a dream? How else could I have awoken screaming because someone is touching me with icy fingers? And it would appear I've had an incontinence episode. (Who said getting old was pretty?)

I try to swat the person away and escape those icy digits, but my arms flail as though I have little control over them. Oh, Lord, did I have a stroke? Please tell me I didn't have a stroke.

I kick my legs to no avail as the cold hands efficiently clean me. It feels like they've put a fresh diaper on me, and someone is wrapping me in blankets again. I'm still screaming for someone to tell me what is going on, but all anyone will say is, "There, there, you're okay."

Although my vision remains blurry, I recognize the face of the woman holding me from earlier, but she is no longer sweaty and mussed. Instead, she is beautifully fresh faced, and her hair is piled high on top of her head. This woman and a man, whom I also recognize from earlier, are talking in quiet voices about packing up their bags and making sure the car seat is strapped in correctly.

Suddenly, the woman looks down at me and asks, "Are you ready to go home, Evelyn?"

I scream, "*No*, not with you people! I want to wake up and go back to my own house with my family!" It seems like I'm not speaking the same language as these two people, though, because they both smile, shush me, and carry me out of the hospital room.

As I'm carried by this woman down a hallway, they are stopped by another couple. This other couple says, "Oh, what a beautiful baby! When was she born?"

The woman holding me says, "Thank you. She was born two days ago at 9:30 p.m. We're naming her Evelyn."

Wait, that is my name! Why would these people say they are naming me my name? The other couple look at each other, and the woman wipes a tear from her eye. "That was my mother's name. She passed away two months ago here in this hospital."

My vision still isn't clear, but this new woman leans close enough that I can see her face. It's my daughter Amelia! She smiles down at me, congratulates the woman holding me, and moves out of sight. The woman holding me smiles down at me.

"Okay, honey. Daddy and I are taking you home now." She puts me in a seat and efficiently buckles the straps. Then she sits next to the seat I'm in as I hear a motor start and feel the motion of riding in a car.

As I ride along next to the woman calling me Evelyn, it occurs to me that I am not dreaming and never was. I couldn't figure out where I was because no one remembers how it feels before being born or how it feels to be born. Even as I realize that I died that night in room

1204 and have been reincarnated, my memories begin to fade. I soon settle into the untroubled sleep of a newborn.

I wonder where my travels will take me next.

Northern Heights

TASSIE KALAS HANEY

*A*fter this, I swore it would be the last time I'd go out on a limb for my kids.

When they were younger and I would announce to them we were going on a family vacation, they would clap and cheer and run off to pack their little Disney suitcases full of their favorite toys. They didn't care where we were going as long as they could stay in a motel with a pool. I was their hero, a young, cool mom with a fold-out map and a picnic basket. They'd cheerfully follow me to the ends of the earth and write about their adventures on postcards they'd send to their envious friends.

But they were older now, and few things were worth writing home about.

I wanted to curse the day I came home from the AAA store armed with travel brochures and a huge smile. It was a gorgeous spring day in Houston, and I had just booked a once-in-a-lifetime trip for my teenaged children, my parents, and me, and I could barely contain myself.

When I walked through the door, my twenty-year-old daughter, Kati, an aspiring photographer in her second year at A&M, paused long enough to look up from her laptop, where she was editing photos. She observed the blue AAA bag in my hand and eyed me suspiciously.

"Please tell me you didn't book anything for July. I'm working every weekend in July."

Her seventeen-year-old sister, Kristina, a high school senior with a perpetual case of spring fever, sensed big news and muted the show she was watching on Netflix. "Hope it's Hawaii! Or Mexico! Any place warm and sunny." She leaped up from the sofa and stretched out her slim frame. "I'm so pale! And I'll need a new swimsuit." She grabbed for the brochure in my hand. "So where are we going, Mom?"

My smile dimmed, but I was determined not to let them dampen my excitement.

"I don't know. Do *Juneau?*" I exaggerated the last word, drawing out the first syllable.

"No," Kristina said, slowly pronouncing each word. "That's why I want to see the *brochure.*"

Kati's lip curled. "Alaska, stupid. She's taking us to Alaska. I bet it's a cruise."

Her younger sister's face fell. "Alaska cruises are for old people." She slumped back down on the sofa, pulled out her cell phone, and began to text, no doubt reporting the unfairness of her life to her best friend. "Boring." She looked up at me and rolled her eyes. "So much for getting a tan."

I tried to hide my disappointment and went into my bedroom to call my mother. She answered on the tenth ring, and I sprung my surprise, knowing I could at least count on her to be thrilled about my gift.

"Alaska?" My mother paused for so long, I thought she had hung up or fainted from excitement. "It's cold in Alaska. And it's for . . ." She hesitated and then whispered, "Old people."

It was then I made the horrifying realization that I had just booked a trip to the only state in the United States that apparently catered to the ninety-something crowd. Worse yet, if I was the only one who thought it sounded fun, maybe I was the old one.

My apprehension only grew in the weeks leading up to the trip. My mother called me daily: to go over what she was packing, to fret over whether her fur coat would be warm enough, or to question where she could purchase long underwear for my dad in July. She packed and repacked gloves and scarves, boots and hats, certain she and my dad would freeze, even though I argued it would be summer in Alaska too.

My daughters, on the other hand, put off packing until the night before. Between the two of them, they brought three mittens and one long-lost hoodie they found in the bottom of the hall closet for warmth, but somehow the weight of their suitcases still managed to exceed the airline's limit.

As we waited in line at the cruise terminal in Seattle, I took on the impossible role of keeping my travel companions happy. The girls were satisfied as long as their cell phones were charged, Wi-Fi was available, and they were receiving an acceptable number of likes on Instagram.

My parents proved to be more challenging.

My dad needed food, and lots of it. My mother required coffee to cope. Both struggled to keep up, barely visible behind the mountain of carry-ons they balanced in their arms. Still, even with their slower pace, neck pillows, and coolers full of medication, I couldn't help noticing they were two of the youngest people in line to embark on the ship.

I had the sinking feeling we were boarding the Titanic.

"This is going to be so much fun!" My cheerful tone sounded fake even to me. I directed everyone to the excursion booth. "Let's book some activities before they're all sold out."

"I'm getting something to eat, and I'm taking a nap." My dad shuffled off in search of the nearest buffet. Broad as a bull and just as strong, his posture read that he was on vacation and he was going to do whatever he wanted, with or without us. He whistled for my mom to follow.

I studied the list of excursions. This would be a fun, memorable vacation if it killed me.

"How about a ride in a vintage railcar through the scenic mountains?"

"Boring!" the girls chimed in unison.

"No trains," my mom called over her shoulder to me as she rushed to catch up with my dad. "Trains are dangerous. Some shopping. Maybe a bus tour of the city."

I examined the ad for the train ride again. *Explore Alaska's Inside Passage and enjoy panoramic views of mountains, glaciers, gorges, and waterfalls*, it read. How much safer could you get? The most challenging part of this excursion would be getting their cabooses all aboard.

"We'll take two tickets for the train." It would do my parents good to get out of their comfort zone for a couple of hours. "Now for us . . ."

"Dogsledding!" Kristina pointed to a picture of a team of huskies pulling a sled through the snow. "The three-hour trip includes flightseeing via helicopter and one hour at a dogsled camp," she read. "And we get to see two glaciers. Now that would be fun!"

"You know I'm afraid of heights." My heart pounded at the thought of boarding a helicopter and almost stopped altogether when I saw the price. "Besides, that excursion costs more than the entire cruise! Let's look for something more reasonable we can all enjoy." I wiped the sweat off my brow with the back of my hand; my eyes begged the excursion director for help.

She pointed to a picture of a family wearing matching helmets and huge smiles. "May I suggest our Alaska Canopy Adventure?" She gave me a subtle once over and erased the beginnings of a smirk off her face. "It's very popular with our younger, more adventurous guests. Entirely safe, of course." She studied my face for a moment. "Unless you'd rather go on the train ride with your parents . . ."

"Alaska Canopy Adventure it is." *Whatever that is.* I pulled out my Visa card and thrust it at the young woman behind the counter. "You only live once!"

I linked arms with the girls as we headed down the long corridor to our cabin, pausing for me to kiss each one gently on the forehead. It took so little to make them happy. My heart soared at the joy I saw on their faces.

"I can't wait for tomorrow! I'm going to get the best photos, ever." Kati looked at me with admiration in her eyes. "I'm so proud of you, Mom. Facing your fears like that."

I froze. "What do you mean?"

"Zip-lining? Tomorrow? Nonrefundable?" She pointed to the tickets I clutched in my hand and read the fine print out loud. "Enjoy the thrill of gliding through the top of a rich rainforest canopy over eight zip lines and three suspension bridges one hundred thirty-five feet above the forest floor." She watched the blood drain from my face. "Mom, are you okay?"

Kristina fanned me with a map of Juneau, her brown eyes wide with concern. "What's there to worry about?" She looked genuinely puzzled. "You'll be wearing a helmet."

The next morning, I woke with a dreadful feeling in my stomach and the metallic taste of terror on my tongue. Two things forced me out of my cozy cabin bed: the mental image of my mother, who I feared I was turning into if I didn't fly out of my comfort zone, and my two pushy daughters, who stood at the foot of my bed, hands on their hips. For once, they were up before me, already dressed for adventure.

Kristina wrestled me out of my bunk, a determined look on her face. "Rise and shine," she sang in her best morning-mom impression. She took in my watery eyes and slumped shoulders. "You literally look like you've just lost your phone, or worse. It's going to be fun."

Kati took over. "Seriously, Mom. I've done this before. You'll be fine." She handed me a cup of coffee and my running shoes. "And we'll get the greatest pictures." Poised and unflappable, she strapped her camera bag over her shoulders and looked me up and down with the critical eye of a photographer. "Is that what you're wearing?"

I took a sip of the scalding coffee, summoned my inner warrior, and eyed the two confident young women in front of me, leaders in Lululemon. I wasn't getting any younger, their expressions read. I'd better live a little while I still could.

I warmed up to the idea as we exited the ship and met the others who were going on the excursion. Everyone was so happy and excited, I almost forgot the fear that simmered deep in my bowels. I even enjoyed the jeep ride through the Tongass National Forest. In my quest to spot a black bear with the other eager tourists, I didn't notice how high we were climbing up the winding roads.

Somehow, I allowed the tour guides—a perky blonde with pigtails and her partner, a hunky bearded lumberjack with a man bun—to slip a leather harness up my legs and around my waist.

In denial, I followed the others up a steep stairway wrapped around a massive trunk until all twelve of us circled the tree, over a hundred feet up, perched on a wooden platform no larger than my coffee table. I clutched the trunk for dear life.

This was taking my love for my children to new heights.

"Wow!" Kati clicked her camera furiously. "The view is amazing!"

"Are those people down there, or ants?" Kristina's laughter rang out through the woods.

"Girls, hold on!" With both arms wrapped around its mighty trunk in a bear hug, I felt the rough bark of the tree against my cheek. My heart pounded as I clung to the spruce and willed myself not to look down. "Don't stand too close to the edge."

I vaguely heard Lumberjack and Jill giving instructions to our group. Then Jack clipped his lanyard onto the pulley and, with a hearty whoop, zipped across the cable, disappearing over the trees. The group chattered excitedly, arguing over who would get to be next. I embraced the tree tighter as one by one Jill sent an ecstatic explorer flying off through the clouds.

"My turn!" I recognized Kristina's excited voice.

I uncurled one finger from the tree. "Don't you dare." My voice came out shaky and hoarse, and the pounding of my heart drowned out my pathetic plea. On land, I would die for my children. Now, all my maternal instincts evaporated as I shamefully realized that if my youngest daughter wanted to take a flying leap off a tree two hundred feet up, I was too concerned about my own safety to come to her rescue. I watched with tears in my eyes as she flew through the air, clutching her cell phone, and her thin frame disappeared in the clouds.

"I'm next!" Kati undid her ponytail and shook her hair free.

Clutching her camera in one hand, she posed for a selfie as Jill clipped her to the cable and gave her a gentle push.

"No!" I hung my head, still clinging tightly to the tree. I would expect my younger, more reckless daughter to throw caution to the wind, but now my careful older one was close behind her.

I hugged the tree tighter, and we swayed softly in the wind, dancing to the rhythmic sounds of the forest. I inhaled its piney cologne and ran my fingers through its mossy mane.

"And last but not least!"

Jill motioned for me to join her at the edge of the platform, but I shook my head and tightened my grip. She reached for my hand and slowly peeled it away from the tree. I resisted, but she was remarkably strong for such a tiny woman.

"You don't want to keep the others waiting, do you?"

And annoying.

"I'll just wait here until you get back," I reasoned, but she shook her head. "I know it's hard to believe, but I'm afraid of heights." I grimaced as she pulled my other arm off the trunk and slowly turned my body to face her.

"There's no turning back now." Jill spoke to me like I was a woman on the verge of a nervous breakdown. Which I was. "I'll be right behind you."

I wrung my hands as she clipped my equipment onto a pulley. "That thing won't hold me!" I glanced back one last time at the safe spot in the shade where my tree and I had shared a warm embrace.

"I think it will." Jill tugged on my harness as if to reassure me.

"I lied about my weight on the waiver!" I blurted out my shameful confession, hoping I would be banned from the park.

She gave me a once over and adjusted a strap. "We know. We added thirty pounds."

Before I could open my mouth to protest, she continued. "Just straighten your legs in front of you and enjoy the view. Remember, slow down by pulling on the cable right before you reach the next platform."

I don't want to die this way! A million thoughts ran through my head. *What if they bury me in some awful dress?* I could hear it now. *What possessed her to do it? She had a beautiful life until she jumped off that tree in Alaska. Wearing some kind of kinky leather harness, no less. I heard she did it for her children. Alaska! Why'd she want to go there, anyway? It's for old people.*

I teetered on the edge of the platform and made the mistake of looking down past my feet, where as far as I could see was sky and trees. My heart leaped into my throat. Then Jill pushed me with all her demonic strength, and I flew through the air.

"Nooooo!"

My anguished scream echoed through the woods. The bright warm day grew dark and chilly for a moment as my harnessed Tongass zipped past the sun. I imagined parents down below shielding their children's eyes from the round globes seeping out of the bottom of my harness. *Don't look directly at it!* they'd shout at the little ones. *You'll go blind!*

The wind took my breath away as I soared through the trees. I made promises to God I had no intention of keeping and recited the Lord's Prayer seven times. Then, miraculously, I spotted something in the distance. My light at the end of the tunnel appeared to me in the shape of a platform. *I might survive, after all, if a branch doesn't impale my inside passage first.*

I squinted. I could make out the form of a man waving his arms, his mouth open as he shouted something.

As I drew nearer, I could see my daughters gesturing frantically at me, reaching up and pulling something over and over again.

"Mom, slow down!"

By the time I made the alarming realization that I was speeding toward Jack with the power of a derailed train, it was too late. The others dived behind the tree trunk for shelter as I flew full force into his spread arms.

The impact of our helmets nearly knocked me out cold. I could feel the splintered texture of the platform under my knees, but something warm and forgiving had broken my fall. I breathed in a musky, woodsy smell. Maybe my worst nightmare had turned into a pleasant dream. I would open my eyes and find I had dozed off on a beach in Hawaii, a romance novel spread open on my tanned tummy.

I tried to speak, but something furry and round gagged my mouth. The figure beneath me squirmed in an enticing way, and I almost didn't want to open my eyes.

"Mom!" Kristina's tone of disapproval was unmistakable.

My eyes flew open. To my horror, I found myself straddling Jack, whose helmet had flown off in our collision. His bite-size man bun was lodged firmly in my mouth.

"I'm okay!" He brushed himself off, reassured everyone, and reshaped his bun.

Sputtering, I staggered to my feet as Kati clicked her camera feverishly. Avoiding the edge of the platform, I raced to the middle and embraced the safety of the tree.

At least I was alive. And more than ready for the free hot chocolate promised in the brochure.

Just then, Jill soared up, landing gracefully on the platform. "Who's ready for zip line number two?"

The others clamored for position in line, each one wanting to be first.

"Wait a minute!" My fear echoed through the forest. "You mean we have to do this again?"

Jack turned his back to me, feigning interest in some pulleys, but Jill looked me directly in the eyes. "We have three more zip lines." She ignored the panic on my face. "And two suspension bridges."

"Look, we signed up to zip-line, and now we've zip-lined," I reasoned with the perky blonde. "It's really not for me, and I'd like to go home." From the corner of my eye, I saw Kati and Kristina wither in unison.

"We're in the middle of the rainforest on a platform." Jill's steely gray eyes bore into mine. "There are only two ways out. You complete the course." Her evil smile sent shivers up my spine. "Or we lower you down on a rope. Someone will come by to pick you up." Her eyes gleamed. "If a bear doesn't first. The choice is yours."

Still clinging to the tree, I looked down. I contemplated

descending the rope of shame, getting stuck all alone, bear bait bobbing in midair, a tasty treat for the first grizzly that ambled by. How I wished I were on that boring train ride, sitting next to my parents, sipping coffee and chatting about my father's sugar level.

Jill nodded with satisfaction when she saw my indecision, then addressed the others. "This is a longer, faster zip line." She paused until the cheering stopped. "So feel free to experiment with some spins."

Jack whooshed off upside down along the cable to ready the next platform for our arrival. The girls jumped up and down in anticipation, planning how they could get the perfect shot of their stunts. My only comfort was the tree gently rocking in my arms.

It'll get better, the others promised, pumped up on adrenaline. *Don't you feel empowered now that you've faced your greatest fear?* But each zip line proved to be more humiliating than the last. In one day, I'd become an avid tree hugger. Only I wasn't saving trees; they were saving me. At each step in the course, Jill would mutter under her breath and unwrap me from my leafy embrace.

Goodbye, tall, bark, and handsome! I'll never fir-get you . . .

Ignoring my protests, she'd clip me onto the next pulley and send me hurling through the sky at breakneck speed. Jack quaked in his hiking boots each time he saw me racing toward him.

The bridges were no better. The others pretended not to enjoy making them wobble to hear my screams.

In fact, the best part of the entire day was landing on the final platform. At last, I could see the ground. My daughters cringed as I kneeled down and kissed the weathered wood. Jack presented each of us with a bronze medal for completing the course and hustled us down to the lodge gift shop.

I sat on a bench sipping hot chocolate and waiting for my knees to stop shaking while the girls shopped. A few minutes later, they walked up wearing matching knit moose caps and handed me a small paper bag.

"What's this?" I pulled out a pair of wool socks with a scene of Alaska on them, a blue glacier stretching up each leg.

"They're for you." Kati grinned. "So you'll never get cold feet again. You really faced your fears up there, Mom."

"I'm not sure which fear I was facing." I felt the texture of the wool in my hand and traced the outline of the glacier with my fingertip. "My fear of heights, or my fear of getting old, of seeming old to you."

I leaned down, changed into my new socks, and wiggled my toes. "Sometimes you get cold feet because you're scared, and maybe that's a good thing. It saves you from doing something dangerous."

The wind picked up and I hugged myself. "And sometimes you get cold feet because it's cold."

We boarded the bus that would take us back to the ship. The girls dozed as I gazed out the window, mesmerized by the view. The tip of the Mendenhall Glacier glistened in the distance, like a blue diamond dropped straight from heaven into a crystal pool of water. The trees lining the road grew lush with leaves, and the bus driver pointed out an eagle soaring overhead. As we circled down the mountain, I could see the ornate caboose of an old train on the tracks below, chugging slowly through the forest.

Maybe my mom was right. A little shopping and a bus tour were all the adventure I needed. I looked forward to seeing my parents that night and sharing stories about our adventures over dinner. I closed my eyes, replaying the day in my head. I may have faced a fear, but I certainly hadn't overcome it.

That's the last time I let my kids talk me into something I don't want to do. No matter how old I am! I nodded off to the humming of the bus motor.

An abrupt stop jolted me awake. A long line of brake lights signaled the road was closed ahead. Sirens wailed in the distance. The driver picked up the microphone and made an announcement to the passengers.

"Sorry for the delay, folks. It seems the White Pass historic train has derailed. We don't know how serious it is yet, but I see lots of ambulances up ahead. We might be here awhile . . ."

I gasped and sat up straighter, trying to get a better view out the window. *Not the train I made my parents go on!* I searched in my backpack for my phone. No service. I woke up the girls, but there was nothing we could do as the bus inched its way through the traffic.

Kristina sobbed against the window, her shoulders gently shaking. "I can see the train down there!" She grabbed my hand. "It doesn't look good."

Whatever you do, don't look down!

Fear and guilt consumed me as I thought of my parents in that wreckage. They would never have been there in the first place if I hadn't shamed them into going. If I hadn't made them feel old.

Take a deep breath.

I willed myself to remain positive. We didn't know where their seats were on that train. Surely not all the cars were part of that tangled mess. I pounded my armrest, but the bus continued to creep along the highway.

When we finally made it to the dock, the girls and I ran all the way to the ship, barely slowing down for security.

I stopped an officer at the entrance of the ship. "The train wreck! My parents . . ."

"Go to the purser's desk." He pointed to a long line snaking through the lobby. "They'll answer your questions." He noticed the panic in my eyes and softened. "There were no casualties."

We joined the others at the back of the line.

"That old couple's been up there for fifteen minutes," a red-faced man growled in front of us. "Hurry up already!"

I looked up to see what couple he was talking about and spotted my mom and dad, holding hands and two cups of coffee, walking away from the desk.

"Who do you think you're calling old?" I pushed past the man and ran up to my parents. "Are you okay?"

"The damn train derailed." My dad shook his head and raised an eyebrow. "But we got them to give you a refund."

"Who cares about the refund? We were so worried about you!" The girls and I hugged the pair, careful not to spill their coffee in our excitement.

"Those poor old people!" My mother clucked her tongue. "You

could never get *me* on that train. Did you see those cliffs in the brochure?"

"What do you mean?" I studied their faces, more confused than ever. "I bought you tickets."

My mother looked down, a sheepish look on her face. "Besides, Albert didn't want to wake up that early. We stayed on board and had a nice lunch on the deck." She beamed at her granddaughters. "Did you girls have a relaxing day?"

My daughters laughed at my expression, and Kati made us all pose for a picture.

"I don't know about you, but I'm hungry." My dad headed in the direction of the dining room with my mother trailing behind.

"Hey, Mom!" Kristina pointed to the excursion desk. Beside it hung a huge poster of a smiling family sitting in an inflatable raft, wearing life jackets and white knuckles. *Enjoy a heart-pounding fourteen-mile trip down Class IV whitewater rapids,* it read. *Guides are certified swift-water rescue technicians!* "What are we doing tomorrow?"

"I'm too old for that!" I made the announcement with pride and hurried to catch up with my parents. I might have been over the hill, but I wanted to live to see a few more mountains.

And suddenly my feet felt cold.

GARY KUNTZ

*E*arly one morning, Hosea, a young man in his late twenties, makes his way through a labyrinth of narrow streets. He walks like someone with a pressing purpose, pushing himself through the crowds of people, for he needs to have a serious talk with his rabbi, who lives in the northern section of the city of Samaria.

When Hosea arrives at his rabbi's house, he gently knocks on the door and waits impatiently. When the rabbi opens his door and sees Hosea standing there, he smiles broadly. "Hey, Hosea. What's up?"

Hosea, not wanting to interrupt his rabbi's busy schedule, asks if he has some time to talk with him.

The rabbi has time, so he happily says, "Sure. Come on in. Pull up some floor. What's on your mind this sunny morning?"

After finding a spot to sit, Hosea hangs his head and rubs his hands together. He's hesitant. He seems to be trying to figure out how to say what he needs to say. All of these are signals that there's something grave, grim even, that troubles him terribly.

After several uncomfortable minutes, Hosea finally speaks. "Rabbi, Yahweh spoke to me yesterday."

"*Really?* What'd He say?"

"Rabbi, you know me, right? I mean, you know I'm not someone who goes around flippantly saying, 'Thus, Yahweh says this' and 'Thus,

Yahweh says that.' You know that even when Yahweh might speak to me, I'm always so doubtful that it is in fact Him speaking. I try very hard to make sure it is Him speaking to me. And what it seems He said to me yesterday befuddles me . . . and scares me. That's why I'm here. I need to talk about this with you."

"Yes, Hosea, I know you're not a false prophet cooking up your own ideas and claiming they're Yahweh's. So what is it? What did Yahweh say to you?"

Hosea rubs his hands together again. When he finally makes eye contact, he blurts out, "Yahweh told me to marry a whore!"

The rabbi is struck by this as if someone sucker punched him, for what Hosea just said is beyond repulsive. But he gathers himself, and trying to be the mature, professional leader he's supposed to be, he speaks in as gentle and as controlled a voice as possible.

"Hosea, Hosea, Hosea. You know what the Scripture teaches. We're not to marry whores; we're to stone them, purging the evil from our midst."

Seeing that Hosea is listening, the rabbi presses a little more. "Hosea, I know you to be a sincere, godly young man. And I know you have no notion to do something stupid, much less sinful. So there is no way Yahweh told you to do this. It just doesn't fit with His Word."

Hosea nods in agreement. "But, Rabbi, I'm not making this up. I'm telling you, I'm pretty sure Yahweh told me to marry a whore. The thing is, I have *no* idea *why* He would tell me to do such a thing, for I do know what the Scripture says about this."

"Hosea, you know I respect you. But I'm telling you, this is just not something Yahweh would tell anyone to do. It's unbiblical."

"I agree, Rabbi. But may I give you an example of an extreme violation of Scripture that Yahweh actually liked?"

"Uh . . . okay . . . sure."

"How about when David brought the Ark of the Covenant to Jerusalem instead of taking it to Gibeon and putting it in the Holy of Holies in the Tabernacle of Moses? Not only did David not return the Ark to its biblically commanded place in the Holy of Holies, but he put the Ark in a tent he set up in his backyard and threw open the flaps, inviting in whosoever wished to worship Yahweh in His Holy Presence. Under penalty of death, only the high priest was allowed to do that, and that only one day a year. Was that not a major and dangerous violation of the clear instructions of the Word of God?"

"Hmm. I forgot David did that. But . . . but this is different. David was passionately pursuing the Living God. His actions, while radical and unbiblical and even dangerous, can actually be praised for just how much he wanted to have the actual Presence with him.[1] But marrying a whore . . ."

"I know, Rabbi. Marrying a whore is despicable, abominable, and thus should be unthinkable. There isn't any obvious righteousness to it, such as hungering for the actual Presence of Yahweh. But I still say that Yahweh told me to do this."

"Well, I know I can't stop you, Hosea. You are your own man, and you get to make your own life choices. Yet I still strongly suggest you make the right choice and put this silly idea out of your mind."

"Here's the bottom line for me, Rabbi: I am hoping to get married someday and have a family. And I know my parents can find me several godly women from which to choose a wife. And that is what I want, as I have no desire to marry a whore. To me, just the idea of talking with a whore is incredibly disgraceful, much less marrying one."

"Now you're making sense, Hosea."

"But, Rabbi, that this idea is so revolting and repulsive to me is the very thing that gives me some confidence that this is not something I cooked up within myself. This had to have come from Yahweh."

"Interesting. I see your point. But I still advise against it."

"I understand, Rabbi. Thanks for your time."

As Hosea rises to leave, the rabbi asks, "What are you going to do?"

"Rabbi, as you have said many times, sometimes faith is spelled r-i-s-k. So I'm going to do what I believe Yahweh told me to do. I'm going to go to the part of town where the whores generally hang out,

---

[1] Psalm 132; Acts 13:22

try to figure out which one I should pick, introduce myself to her, and see what happens."

"Well, please know that no matter what happens, I'm still your rabbi and friend. Shalom."

"Peace to you also, Rabbi."

As Hosea is leaving, he stops at the door and turns around. "Rabbi, when I find the right whore, will you do the marriage ceremony?"

The rabbi ponders this for a moment. "Uh . . . sure. But what about the eight-week premarital counseling course I do with couples?"

"I guess if she's willing to marry me, she'll probably be willing to attend your premarital counseling course."

"Good. That will at least give me a chance to strongly stress the issue of being faithful to one's husband."

"Yeah. Good idea. I would *really* appreciate that. Thanks."

Hosea leaves.

That evening, Hosea makes his way to *that* part of town. He has never done anything like this before. Ever!

He wonders what he's supposed to talk about with a whore. Or should he forget the getting-to-know-her part and just jump right in and ask her to marry him?

I can't just say, 'Hi, my name is Hosea. Will you marry me?' What's she going to say? 'Oh, you poor kid. You've never done this before, have you? Look, we're just going to have sex; we're not going to get married! In fact, I'm not even going to be your girlfriend. This is business. We have sex . . . and you pay me for it. Of course, you can get on my Elite Member's Plan and become one of my steady customers. But marriage? Oh no, no, no!'

Hosea sighs, "Ugh. I really don't want to do this."

As Hosea plays these various scenarios and conversations in his head, he slowly makes his way to a place where music is playing, people are having conversations, and of course, clinking cups are flowing with plenty of wine.

As he stands in the doorway of one of these places, he tries to rally some resolve by reminding himself that he's pretty sure Yahweh has told him to marry a whore. Quickly, he scans the room, and as he does, he sees a particular woman sitting and talking with some people at a table in the corner. Even in the low light, Hosea can see there is just something about her gentle eyes and simple smile. Trying to appear confident, he walks over to this little group, makes eye contact with this particular woman, clears his throat, and shyly says, "Hello, my name is Ho . . . ho . . . Hosea."

All stop talking, for they all know there is a rookie in the house. But the woman smiles an open, friendly smile with her entire face. "Hi, I'm Gomer. What can I do for you?"

Instantly, Hosea is struck by this woman's eyes, and maybe he remembers what Solomon penned of the Bridegroom's words about His Bride's eyes:

> **You have ravished my heart, my bride; you have stolen my heart with one glance of your eyes. Turn your eyes from me; they overwhelm me.**[2]

After this first encounter, Hosea visits with Gomer many times, talking late into the night. And although she initially gives him quite obvious overtures to have sex, using her well-practiced approaches of wanton touches, tantalizing scents, and her best come-hither looks, these overt tactics slowly give way until she stops them completely, for she comes to respect Hosea, realizing he has no desire for empty sexual encounters.

As Hosea and Gomer's relationship develops, Gomer confides how, from a young age, she has dreamed that a godly man would come into her life, wed her, and have a family with her. And she really means this; it isn't silly chatter, for she truly wants a loving husband, several children, and the sense of home and family.

With conversations like these, it isn't long before Hosea begins falling genuinely in love with Gomer. *Profoundly* in love. Hosea opens his heart wide and deep and high and loves Gomer with everything he

---

[2] Song of Songs 4:9a, 6:5a

has in him with which to love a woman. When he asks her to marry him, she, in disbelief at her good fortune, throws her arms around his neck, tears of joy filling her eyes.

"Oh my God! Yes, yes, yes!"

Then, for the first time, they kiss. It is not some quick peck on the lips, but a longing kiss. A kiss of love.

And when they kiss, maybe another passage from Solomon's Song comes into Hosea's mind, in which Solomon expressed the Bride's passion for her Bridegroom:

Kiss me—full on the mouth! Yes! For your love is better than wine.[3]

When Gomer agrees to marry him, Hosea assumes that all Yahweh must have wanted was for Hosea to experience seeing Him restore a sinner. Maybe this whole "marry a whore" issue was just about a wayward woman repentantly returning to Yahweh.

In his infectious enthusiasm, Hosea goes to see his rabbi, to tell him the really, really, really good news of the miracle of all miracles done by Yahweh to give him the love of his life, who is ready to be wed!

Smiling more widely than his face can hold, Hosea says, "So, Rabbi, Gomer has agreed to marry me! I am giddy and giggly. I can't help it. I am happy, happy, happy! Pinch me; I must be dreaming. This is just too remarkable!"

"Wow. I can see that. That's great, Hosea. And I'm glad this is working out so well for you both. Gomer seems to have turned out to be a quality young woman. Surely she will make you a loving and faithful wife."

"Rabbi, Gomer is beyond my ability to put into words. I don't know what it is, but I am *so* in love with her! And it's not about

---

[3] Song of Songs 1:2

physical beauty. It's not even her personality. I'm lost for words here other than to say . . . I love her because I chose to love her!"

"Again . . . wow! What a beautiful thing, Hosea, for you sound exactly like Yahweh in what He said of Israel.[4] And so, I'm honored to have some small part in putting the two of you together in the covenant of marriage."

Shortly thereafter, they hold the wedding ceremony, but it is not a small, private ceremony with just the couple's families. Instead, many in the city are in attendance, for they all want to celebrate this incredible miracle Yahweh has performed by putting Hosea, a godly young man, and Gomer, a once-prodigal young woman, together as husband and wife.

There is much dancing and celebrating!

Not long after the week-long wedding celebration, Hosea and Gomer settle into the rhythm of married life and daily work.

And one day, not too long after that, Gomer has something she can't wait to tell Hosea, something she can hardly contain. At first, she toys with him, acting quite coy. Finally, smiling with her mouth and her eyes as she usually does and bubbling with overflowing joy, she announces, "My husband, I'm pregnant!"

"What?" Hosea replies in disbelief, almost as if he doesn't know how such a thing could have happened.

As the overwhelming wonderfulness of what Gomer has just revealed seeps into Hosea, his heart explodes with ecstatic elation! After giving Gomer a great big hug and a long, passionate kiss, he takes off running to his rabbi's house, not stopping even once to catch his breath, for he must tell him this fantastically good news.

Breathing heavily from his race, Hosea says, "Rabbi . . . Rabbi . . ." Pausing to try to catch his breath, he adds, "Good news . . . Rabbi! Gomer . . . Gomer . . . is . . . is . . . pregnant!"

---

[4] Deuteronomy 7:6–9

"*Really?* That's awesome!"

The rabbi gives Hosea a hearty slap on the back and a quick manly bear hug. After these masculine acts of affection, he breaks out a couple of cigars and fills a couple of cups with wine.

"Truly, Hosea, Yahweh has blessed you. I am also so glad you didn't listen to me and that you took the risk of obeying what Yahweh told you to do. Way to go, man!"

"Rabbi, I tell you, every morning I wake up with such gratitude that I am married to such an incredible woman. And now, Yahweh adds blessing to blessing by giving us a child! I don't know if I can stand to be this happy!"

Then both men grin toothy grins and share another quick manly bear hug. They both light up their cigars, filling the room with puffy smoke, and just before downing a swig of wine, they lift their glasses high and in unison shout, "L'Chaim!"[5]

Some seven months and eight days later, family and friends are gathered to rejoice with Hosea and Gomer as their baby boy is initiated into the Abrahamic Covenant by circumcision. The rabbi and the mohel of course are also present. As the singing and the prayers come to an end in this sacred ceremony, the mohel asks Hosea what name he has for this baby boy.

Hosea looks down at the ground. Gomer is clearly trying not to make eye contact with anyone. There is instantly some tenseness in the air as Hosea is plainly disturbed.

The rabbi queries, "Hosea. What's wrong? C'mon, just tell us the boy's name."

Hosea raises his head and looks into his rabbi's eyes. In Hosea's eyes, the rabbi can see a sense of sadness, and suddenly a shiver goes down his spine. Then Hosea speaks in a quiet voice, precisely pronouncing each word.

---

[5] *ch* as in the word *loch*

"Yahweh says our son's name is to be Jezreel—because Yahweh will soon punish the house of Jehu for the massacre at Jezreel and He will put an end to the kingdom of Israel."

Stunned silence saturates the room.

A heaviness envelops everyone in attendance. A frightening foreboding makes people's skin crawl. To some few, there is no question that this is a true prophetic word Hosea has delivered, so just those few accept it. But most consider this word a false word because it is just so negative. Surely Yahweh would never do anything so deliberately disciplinary![6]

By that evening, most everyone in the city of Samaria has heard about what happened that morning at the circumcision ceremony for Hosea and Gomer's firstborn son. And by the end of the week, people for miles around have also heard about this prophetic word.

A few make plans to repent, to clean up their lives, to live in the way Yahweh asked them to live—that of a faithful, lovesick bride. The thought that Yahweh would "put an end to the kingdom of Israel" is truly frightening . . . but just to a very few.

As for the vast majority, they believe this is nothing more than some silly man claiming Yahweh spoke to him. Most ignore Hosea's message and go on living as they have been.

The reality is, the truth is, Yahweh . . . is a jealous Husband! He will not share His Wife with anyone or anything. He wants to be loved, and He will do whatever it takes to have such a faithful and lovesick bride.

Many months pass without any sign of judgment, without any actions on the part of Yahweh to do what Hosea said He was going to do to the kingdom of Israel. Most people take such inaction by Yahweh the

---

6 Proverbs 3:11–12

wrong way, thinking He didn't really mean what He told Hosea. Thus, the people went on living in ways that displeased Yahweh.[7]

Then one morning, Hosea shows up at his rabbi's front door. He's smiling, for which the rabbi is relieved.

"Hey, Hosea, what's up?"

Hosea replies, "Rabbi, I have some good news, some very good news." (The rabbi is thinking, *Thank God, some good news!*) "My beautiful wife, who I love so very much, is pregnant. Yes, pregnant . . . again! Yahweh is adding to our little family, Rabbi!"

"That is wonderful, Hosea! I am so happy for you!"

And the rabbi is happy for Hosea. He wants to be even happier. He wants this nagging cloud of judgment to finally stop hovering over him. But right now, he's just glad that Hosea actually said the words, "I have some good news." For these words give him some relief from the relentless pressure of conviction that has been pressing down on his head and shoulders, making the muscles in his neck tense and jittery. He is hopeful that maybe, just maybe, things have gotten better, that maybe Yahweh has relented.

The rabbi smiles back at Hosea. "Well, time to pull out the cigars and, even though it's still early, a little glass of schnapps, something to warm our insides." As he gathers the cigars and pours the schnapps, he continues. "Truthfully, Hosea, you are a fortunate man. You have a beautiful wife, a son, and now another child on the way. Yahweh is blessing you!"

"I don't know what I've done for Yahweh to bless me with such a wife as Gomer, Rabbi. I tell you, I love her utterly."

The rabbi man-hugs Hosea. He's relieved by the easing of the weight of deep concern he's been carrying for himself, his family, and his nation, but he's also happy for Hosea and Gomer and the coming birth of a second child. He and Hosea grin at each other and together exclaim "Mazel tov!" before they swallow the slightly intense liquid.

---

[7] Ecclesiastes 8:11

Approximately six or seven months later, family, friends, and the rabbi gather again for a ceremony celebrating the recent birth of a baby girl to Hosea and Gomer.

Naturally, everyone wants to know what name Hosea will give to his daughter, hoping of course for something upbeat and cheerful. The rabbi, being the acknowledged leader of the group, asks, "So . . . Hosea . . . what will you name your beautiful little girl?"

No sooner have the words exited the rabbi's mouth than, once again, he immediately senses a weightiness filling the room.

As for Hosea, his head is yet again hanging down, his eyes are yet again looking down, and his shoulders are yet again bending down. Gomer too is visibly unhappy; she has closed her eyes, as if trying to make herself disappear. When the rabbi sees this, fear begins to choke him. He wonders where the air went, for he's having trouble breathing.

After a long, uncomfortable pause, Hosea finally makes eye contact with the rabbi. Then he looks at Gomer, for he is very aware of her displeasure with what he must say next. He then looks back at the rabbi and says, with no hesitancy in his tone, "The girl's name is to be Not-Loved, for Yahweh says He will no longer show His Love to Israel."

What's supposed to be a joyous celebration has—yet again— turned sour and sullen. Once again, by that evening, most everyone in the city of Samaria has heard what Hosea prophesied. By the end of the week, people for miles around have also heard it.

Because nothing bad happened from the first prophetic word Hosea gave at his firstborn son's circumcision, this time even fewer people give any credence to Hosea's words. Most believe he is an idiot at the best or a foolish false prophet at the worst. Yahweh would never do something so cruel as to not show His Love to His people, most rationalize.[8]

---

[8] Hebrews 12:5–9

The next day, unable to take the growing angst and hoping for even a little relief, the rabbi seeks out Hosea. When he finds him, he gets right to the point. "Hosea, I love you, man, and I respect you. But the two prophetic words you've given . . . well . . . they're tough to take."

"I know. Believe me, I know. I don't like them myself. I mean, I really do not like them! But even worse, Rabbi, why does Yahweh keep waiting until the birth of one of my children to speak to me? Even more, why is He having me name my precious children these terrible names? What are they going to think when they're older and realize the meaning of their names! Why, Rabbi, why is Yahweh doing this to me?"

"I don't know, Hosea. Although I don't like these words, my sense is that they are right . . . even though they're hard to hear."

Some many more months go by.

Then one day, reluctantly but dutifully, Hosea trudges to his rabbi's house. He knocks on the door and waits. When the rabbi opens the door and sees Hosea standing there, he greets him, also reluctantly but dutifully, as well as with some apprehension.

"Hey, Hosea."

In a just-the-facts tone, Hosea says, "I came to tell you . . . that Gomer . . . my wife who I love so very much . . . is pregnant again."

The rabbi almost blurts out, "Oh no! Not *again!*" But he doesn't. He knows that wouldn't be polite. Instead, he stammers trying to say the polite thing, which still exposes how he feels about the news. "Uh . . . well . . . that's good." Mustering an insincere smile, he adds, "Congratulations."

Hosea looks at the rabbi knowingly. "Thank you, but you know what I'm thinking, don't you?"

The rabbi's head drops. "Yes." Then, looking up at Hosea, he says, "But maybe it will be different this time. Maybe Yahweh is done giving you these hard messages." Trying to say something optimistic, he continues. "Maybe this child will have a name of blessing, something like I-Was-Just-Kidding."

Some seven months and eight days later, the rabbi and the mohel, Hosea and Gomer, their families, and only a few friends are gathered for a third time to conduct the ceremony of circumcision for a baby boy. They all have come out of obligation, for none want to be there. They are all fairly frightened as they halfheartedly sing the songs and pray the prayers associated with the ceremony. Even the mohel is nervous as he asks what name Hosea wants to give this baby boy.

This time, Hosea does not look down. This time, he does not hesitate. This time, he answers in a clipped voice, "His name, Yahweh says, will be Not-My-People, 'for Israel is not My people, and I am no longer their higher power.'"

Woe! It's as if the sound of a judge's hammer slams down at the end of this declared judgment: guilty and rejected! Like the rapid hammering of a jackhammer, the phrase "not My people" pounds again and again in everyone's ears.[9]

It's . . . it's . . . it's as if Yahweh is divorcing His Wife, Israel, due to her idolatrous adultery.

Hosea then turns to Gomer and puts his arms around her as sad tears flow freely down her soft, beautiful cheeks. She hardens her heart as Hosea says, "Honey. You know I love you. And you know I love our children too. You know I would never do anything to purposely hurt any of you. And yet, you know I must say what Yahweh tells me to say."

Gomer doesn't hear him.

---

[9] Jeremiah 23:29

Life has settled down since Hosea's last word, helped by the fact that there haven't been any more messages from Yahweh through Hosea . . . so far.

Then late one night, there is a hard, relentless pounding at the rabbi's door. He, his wife, and their children are already in bed, and he really doesn't want to get out from under the comfortable covers. But the pounding is adamant. There's no way he can ignore this, so before the noise can wake his children, he gets up, goes to the door, and opens it.

Hosea is standing there.

He's shaking, and not because of the cool night's temperature.

His eyes swell with tears that spill out in big droplets and splat upon the ground.

His lips quiver as he tries to say something, but he doesn't seem able to find his voice.

Clearly, something is seriously wrong.

Immediately, the rabbi thinks Hosea has another message. A message so important that he couldn't wait 'til morning to tell it.

Afraid to ask, the rabbi asks, "Hosea, what is it?"

Hosea tries to say something . . . but he can't.

All of a sudden, Hosea collapses to the ground. He's there at the rabbi's front door on his hands and knees. Convulsing, he sobs . . . and sobs . . . and sobs—deep sobs.

The rabbi bends down and puts his hands on Hosea. "What's wrong? What's going on?"

Hosea shudders, weeping harder and harder with cries of anguish. He clearly cannot speak. He cannot even catch his breath. All he can do is wail. Then he painfully inhales a deep breath and exhales a long terrible groan of grief.

The rabbi tries to provide some comfort. He wraps his arms around Hosea, holding him tightly in his agony. Then the rabbi just waits . . . and waits . . . and waits for Hosea to move through his pain so he can explain why he is so crushed, so brokenhearted.

Finally, Hosea says, "Rabbi . . . she's . . . gone."

"Gone? Who's gone?"

"Gomer."

"Gomer? What do you mean, she's gone? You mean she went out for a walk? You mean she went over to her parents' for a little while? What do you mean, she's gone?"

"She's left, Rabbi. She went back to her life as a whore."

"*What?* No way! Are you sure? It can't be!"

"I saw where she went, Rabbi. I saw her with a man, a man we both know. I saw him lustfully take her in his arms and do what only she and I should do. And I could see that she enjoyed it. Rabbi . . . this hurts *so* much! Why? Why would Gomer do this? Why? Why would she shun me and my love? Why? Why would she be *so* unfaithful to someone who loves her *so* much?"

The rabbi has no answer.

However, the rabbi wonders: Is Israel, Yahweh's Wife, doing what Gomer is now doing in spite of how much Hosea has loved her? Is Hosea feeling what Yahweh feels when He sees His Wife loving other lovers in idolatrous adultery? And as a result, has this process that Yahweh put Hosea through made him not only a messenger with a mere message of theology but rather a messenger filled with Prophetic Pathos?[10]

The rabbi remembers how several years back the prophet Amos warned Israel of righteous judgment and Israel ignored that message. The rabbi thinks, *Maybe this entire thing that Hosea has been through has been Yahweh preparing him to make His final appeal—from His heart—to Israel with the message of His* chesed *[11]—His passionately loyal, uncompromising Holy Love.*

---

[10] For the answer to this question, read the Book of Hosea, chapter 2.

[11] *ch* as in the word *loch*

Hosea eventually disciplines and restores Gomer as his wife, a prophetic act declaring that one day Yahweh, after disciplining His Wife, Israel, will restore her.[12] For there is a Day coming in which the Bridegroom-King, the son of David, will return for His Bride and, with her, create a whole new world.

---

[12] Romans 11:25–29

About the Authors

Monica Berry is an award-winning nonfiction and memoir writer. She wrote the weekly column Love Convection for the *Dallas Observer*'s food blog *City of Ate* (available at http://www.dallasobserver.com /authors/monica-berry-6436767). Monica has also appeared in the storytelling shows *Oral Fixation* and *Listen to Your Mother* reading her own work. When she's not writing or storytelling for fun, Monica practices law as the general counsel of an educational software company. A list of all her publications and honors can be found here: https://www.linkedin.com/in/monica-berry-3a1aa33.

Tassie Kalas Haney (Houston, Texas) writes humorous stories about growing up and growing older, looking in the mirror and laughing without fear of the future. Her stories have been published in *Quill and Spark*, *The Ocotillo Review*, and *Laugh Out Loud: 40 Women Humorists Celebrate the Then and Now, Before They Forget*. She was a participant in the Southeast Texas *Listen to Your Mother* show and is a member of the Houston Writers Guild. Visit her at tassietypes.com.

About the Authors

Shane Healy has been writing stories since childhood. When he was sixteen, Shane won a national essay contest hosted by Scholastic and received an all-expenses-paid trip to Edinburgh, Scotland, to meet J. K. Rowling. He is twenty-six years old and is a professional photographer who specializes in portraiture and real estate photography.

Gary Kuntz spent fifteen years in the pastoral ministry, but since 1996 he has been a Special Education teacher assigned to a high school English department. He has written thirteen books related to Christian issues, as well as three children's books.

Arthur Pike is an emerging writer who's been practicing the writing craft in professional and personal settings for several decades. He recently completed a collection of short stories, *The Size of the World We Don't Know*, and is focused on completing a young adult novel with his brother. He lives with his family in Houston, Texas.

Lee Ann Rozek is a Registered Nurse, bookworm, sci-fi/fantasy fan, and mom to an eleven-year-old son. She lives in Tomball, Texas, and grew up in the region. Her interests are varied, and she looks forward to continuing her writing endeavors.

Dorothy Tinker grew up dreaming of fantastical worlds and creatures, of plots in space, and of strange new cultures. After studying mathematics in university, she rediscovered her true passion and rededicated herself to her literary dreams.

Since then, Dorothy has published an ongoing series of young adult spiritual /fantasy novels, including *Peace of Evon*, *Gift of War*, and *Lost King*. Her short stories have appeared in HWG Press's *Riding the Waves* and *Out of Many, One*, Inklings Publishing's *Eclectically Cosmic*, *Eclectically Heroic*, and *Eclectically Magical*, Writespace's *In Medias Res*, and Balance of Seven's *Rogues and Wild Fire*. Her poetry has been published in OWS's *Primal Elements*.

Dorothy is also the co-owner of Balance of Seven literary alliance and owner of D Tinker Editing. She works as copy editor and formatter for Inklings Publishing.

When not writing or finding legal citations for briefs, **Sage Webb** and her husband spend all their time and treasure keeping their mahogany trawler home named *Peregrine* afloat. If *Peregrine* grants them shore leave, they go stand-up paddling, surfing, diving, or climbing. Living on boats and in RVs has given Sage fodder for stories, and her debut novel follows an abused kid from Michigan to a thirty-foot sailboat on Galveston Bay to a federal prison cell: *The Unremarkable Circumstances of Inmate 17656-090* won a Texas manuscript contest before Martin Brown released it in 2018. Sage's short stories have won recognition in the US and UK, and Sage writes for a Gulf Coast magazine, belongs to International Thriller Writers and Read Local, and was thrilled to be on a writing-as-activism panel at the 2018 Writefest. The only thing that could make life better would be having more cats.

About the Judges

When not writing or working her full-time job, **Andrea Barbosa** travels in search of history, museums, and adventures. Her short stories and poems have appeared in several anthologies and journals, including the *Southern Pacific Review* and *Ariel Chart*. Her poetry collection, *Holes in Space*, won the 2015 Reader's Favorite Silver Medal and her Flash Fiction piece, "The Queen of Carnival," won the 2016 Spider's Web Prize from Spider Road Press. She has earned other accolades in flash fiction and romance.

Andrea also writes award-winning romance under the pseudonym Andrya Bailey.

She currently serves as VP and Press Director for the Houston Writers Guild and as Flash Fiction Editor for *The Ocotillo Review Literary Journal*.

Follow her on Twitter: @andyb0810

Educated at University of North Texas, **Tony Burnett** is Managing Editor at Kallisto Gaia Press, home of *The Ocotillo Review* and *The Texas Poetry Calendar* (beginning in 2018). An award-winning poet, journalist, activist, and songwriter, his poetry and short fiction have been published in national literary magazines and anthologies including *Sixfold*, *Connotation Press*, *Short Story America*, *Frontier Tales*, *Texas Poetry Calendar*, *Poetry @ Round Top* anthology, *Tidal Basin Review*, *Di-verse-city*, and *Toucan Literary Magazine*. He is Editor in Chief of *Scribe*, the online blog with over 6,000 subscribers and serves as Board President of the Writers League of Texas. He makes his home in rural central Texas near Temple with his trophy wife, Robin. His hobbies include poking wasp nests with short sticks and wandering aimlessly about.

Currently available: story collection *Southern Gentlemen* (2015 Kallisto Gaia Press), poetry collection *The Reckless Hope of Scoundrels* (May 2016 Kallisto Gaia Press).

Van G. Garrett is the winner of the 2017 Best Book of African American Poetry for his book *49: Wings and Prayers*, as announced by the Texas Association of Authors. Garrett is a poet and fiction writer. He is the author of *Songs in Blue Negritude* (poetry), *ZURI: Selected Love Songs* (poetry), *The Iron Legs in the Trees* (fiction), *49: Wings & Prayers* (poetry), *LENNOX IN TWELVE* (poetry), and *HOG* (poetry). Additionally, Van's poetry and art have been featured and exhibited around the world. His updates and appearances can be found at www.vanggarrett poet.com.

About the Designers

Cover Design

Dylan Drake started Wayword Author Services because she is passionate about helping independent authors. With over 15 years of experience as a graphic designer, she has worked in publishing as well as web design and social media throughout her career. Not only can she help with book cover design, interior book design, editorial, and e-book formatting, but she can create and manage a simple author website and integrate your social media and email campaigns. She designed, edited, and self-published a YA sci-fi series authored by her mother, J.D. Lakey, and she knows the ins and outs of the most popular print-on-demand platforms and e-book distributors. Give her a call today to see how she can help you make your book shine!

Copyediting and Formatting

Dorothy Tinker started D Tinker Editing with a love of language and a keen eye for details. As a published author herself, she understands the personal nature of any writer's work and strives to help each client's words and style shine. D Tinker Editing offers services such as developmental editing, copyediting, proofreading, and formatting. For more information or a price quote, please email dtinker@balanceof seven.com.

TxAuthors.com
A Family of Nonprofits that Support & Market Texas Authors.

DearTexas.Info

Blog Talk
Radio, plus
SoundCloud
& iTunes

**Texas Authors Institute
of History, Inc.**

A Museum that saves Texas Authors
History and Promotes Education in
Reading & Writing.

TexasAuthors.Institute